KILL CREATURES

BY RORY POWER

Wilder Girls
Burn Our Bodies Down
Kill Creatures
In a Garden Burning Gold
In an Orchard Grown from Ash

KILL CREATURES

RORY POWER

DELACORTE PRESS

Delacorte Press
An imprint of Random House Children's Books
A division of Penguin Random House LLC
1745 Broadway, New York, NY 10019
penguinrandomhouse.com
GetUnderlined.com

Text copyright © 2025 by Rory Power
Jacket art copyright © 2025 by Kei-Ella Loewe
Jacket design by Liz Dresner
Map art copyright © 2025 by Mike Hall

Penguin Random House values and supports copyright. Copyright fuels creativity, encourages diverse voices, promotes free speech, and creates a vibrant culture. Thank you for buying an authorized edition of this book and for complying with copyright laws by not reproducing, scanning, or distributing any part of it in any form without permission. You are supporting writers and allowing Penguin Random House to continue to publish books for every reader. Please note that no part of this book may be used or reproduced in any manner for the purpose of training artificial intelligence technologies or systems.

Delacorte Press is a registered trademark and the colophon is a trademark of Penguin Random House LLC.

Library of Congress Cataloging-in-Publication Data is available upon request.
ISBN 978-0-593-30231-6 (trade) — ISBN 978-0-593-30232-3 (lib. bdg.)
ISBN 978-0-593-30233-0 (ebook) — ISBN 979-8-217-11681-2 (international ed.)

Interior design by Ken Crossland
The text of this book is set in 12-point Scala Pro.

Manufactured in the United States of America
10 9 8 7 6 5 4 3 2 1

The authorized representative in the EU for product safety and compliance is Penguin Random House Ireland, Morrison Chambers, 32 Nassau Street, Dublin D02 YH68, Ireland, https://eu-contact.penguin.ie.

Random House Children's Books supports the First Amendment and celebrates the right to read.

For Spencer Hastings, her field hockey stick,
and the kicky little beret she wears in Season 1

A list of content warnings for *Kill Creatures*
is available at the back of this book,
following the acknowledgments,
and on the author's website.

> O, be swift—
>
> we have always known you wanted us.
>
> —H.D., "THE HELMSMAN"

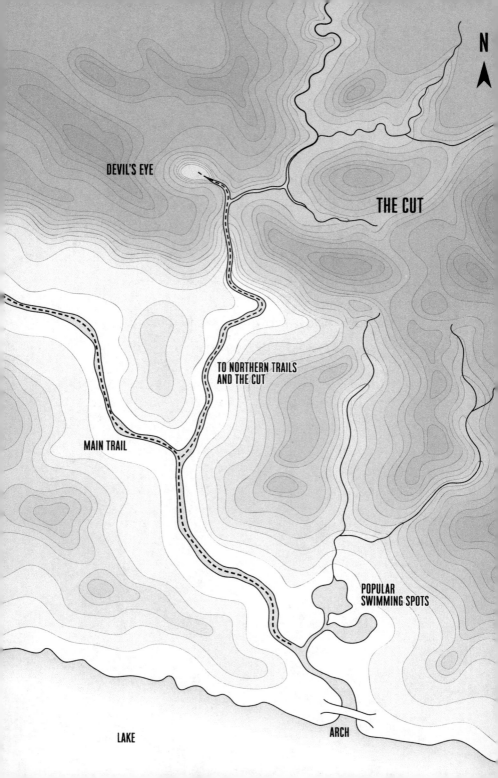

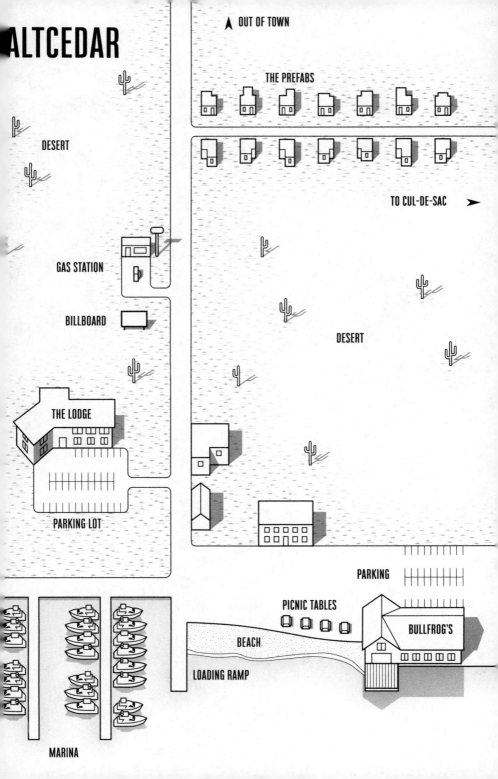

NOW

Start with this, with a bruise-blue sky. Then the clouds gathered low on the horizon, their bellies bloodshot with sunset. And last, the billboard frame and the picture stretched across it: three girls wearing summer smiles. Edie, Jane, and Luce. My best friends, my favorites. Saltcedar's, too, now that they're gone.

For the first few days after they put the billboard up, there was almost always someone here in its shadow. Praying, sometimes, or leaving behind wildflower bouquets. Today it's just me, heat rippling off the road as I balance astride my bike. I came to say goodbye. To take a moment for the four of us before it's all lit candles and bullshit speeches down at the vigil.

"You'd hate it," I whisper to them. The crowds, the

noise. The marina's too busy to launch from. And you need reservations at Bullfrog's now; tourists steal our table every night.

I know some people are happy about it. It's the most activity the town has seen in years. Finally, Saltcedar looks like the pictures in those brochures—sunburned teenagers in life jackets, little kids diving off the backs of houseboats while their parents watch from the upper decks, drinks in hand. But these people don't care that the lake is going dry. They don't care that there's a half-built neighborhood abandoned at the end of my street. They just care that a year ago exactly, my best friends wandered into the dark and let Saltcedar Canyon swallow them whole.

A shaft of sunlight sneaks past the corner of the billboard. I lift a hand to block it. Blink hard as the gas station beyond swims into focus. Through the window, I can see Glen at the register, his face lit up red by the Budweiser sign on the wall. He's wearing one of the T-shirts that the vigil volunteers have been handing out all week. Same picture as the billboard printed across his chest, same text underneath: Bring Them Home. He's probably about to close up and head down to the lake. I'd better hurry, or I'll be one of the last to arrive.

I kick off on my bike. Listen to the crunch of grit under the tires. Glance back at my street, dotted with prefab houses, then keep straight toward the rest of town. Coast easy and free down the hill, eyes drifting shut. If I listen hard, I can feel the girls with me, the air curving around their bodies. They're everywhere. In the lodge lobby, Jane waving as the elevator doors close between her and us. On my front steps, Edie's head bent over her phone as she waits for me to do up my laces. At the water's edge, Luce pointing toward the canyon arch.

Somewhere behind me, a car engine rumbles, getting closer. I swing to the side and pedal harder. None of those memories will count for much if I'm late.

The lodge is off to the right, parking lot already almost full with out-of-state plates. A man I don't recognize is waiting near the entrance next to a table stacked high with candles. I ignore the one he holds out to me. Keep going, slip between two pickups toward the far side of the lot where Mr. and Mrs. Bristow are standing, sweat patches stark against their white vigil T-shirts.

It's been a while since I've seen Jane's parents in person, but some things haven't changed. The sunscreen on Mr. Bristow's forehead, not quite rubbed in. The glint of Mrs. Bristow's wedding ring as she twists it absently around her knuckle. She's got her hair pulled back—heavy and dark like her daughter's. Jane used to lie out in the boat as we drifted, her hair spread long and gleaming over Luce's lap. Gathering sunlight in its strands until it was too hot to touch.

I leave my bike leaning against somebody's back bumper. Wipe my clammy palms dry on my shorts before I close the last gap between me and Jane's parents. "Hi," I say, skirting another group of volunteers. "Sorry, I know I'm late."

Mr. Bristow sees me first. "Not at all," he says, and waves me closer. "You're right on time."

Next to him, Mrs. Bristow doesn't look up. She's poring over a clipboard, her mouth moving silently as she reads something off it. Her speech for the vigil, maybe. Is she nervous? Sure, there'll be cameras there, reporters and news trucks, but you'd think she'd be used to that after the press tour she and her husband have done on Jane's behalf.

Mr. Bristow nudges her. "Carrie? Carrie, it's Jane's friend."

"Hmm?" She meets my eyes, and for a moment I think she doesn't recognize me, but then she blinks, seems to wake from a long midnight. "Oh, Nan. You're here."

She wraps me up in a hug. I lean in, let her tuck my head against her neck the way she might if I were Jane. Is she remembering the same thing I am? Six or seven summers back, me waiting in the shade with my dad to meet Mom after her shift at the lodge front desk. Jane climbing out of the Bristows' rental SUV, her mother's words carrying across the pavement: "See, there's a girl your age."

Jane waved at me then. It took me days to work up the nerve to wave back.

"It's good to see you, sweetheart," she says as she releases me. "Gosh, were you this tall last summer?"

"I think so." I smile uneasily. She's doing her best to seem normal, but her eyes are red and her voice is hoarse. It's painfully obvious she's been crying. I look away, gesture to the crowd. "This is all . . . There's so many people here for them. You must be really pleased."

"Of course," Mr. Bristow says. "It's a testament to the girls."

"Is there anything you need?" Mrs. Bristow asks, all but interrupting him. There's a hunger in her stare, like she wishes she hadn't let go of me. "We have water and sunblock over by the lodge entrance, and— Oh, you need a T-shirt." She flags down a passing volunteer. "Can we get Nan a shirt? What size are you, honey? A medium? Let's get you a medium, yeah."

Moments later a T-shirt is thrust into my hands, so fresh out of the box that the creases where it was folded are still sharp. I crumple it up against my ribs. Make sure I can't see any of the girls' faces.

"Thanks," I say. "I'll change before the marina."

"Speaking of," Mr. Bristow interjects, "we should head down. The Gales are already there."

I'm not surprised they aren't here with the Bristows.

Edie's parents used to get along so well with Jane's. In those first few months after the girls disappeared, they did everything as a quartet—every interview, every press conference. But Saltcedar rich isn't Salt Lake City rich. Before long, it was only the Bristows flying to New York and LA. Only the Bristows appearing on national TV, only Jane that anyone was talking about. I don't think the Gales would ever admit to being angry, but they don't have to; everybody knows they are anyway.

Still, it could be worse. At least they tried. Luce's dad couldn't even do that.

"What about Mr. Allard?" I ask. "Is he here?"

Mrs. Bristow's smile goes stiff, her eyes darting to the crowd milling around us. "Kent was invited," she says, too politely. "I'm not sure he'll be able to make it, though."

I think we're all hoping he won't. Whenever Kent Allard shows up, he brings trouble with him. Shouting, crying. Stories and ghosts and the smell of alcohol.

I guess I understand it. Luce's mom left spring of last year, and then Luce disappeared that summer. Both Allard women gone by the time the cold came, and Kent so ruined by it that even the police left him alone after a while.

Mr. Bristow's hand lands on my shoulder for a second, startling me. "What about your parents, Nan? I don't think I've seen them yet."

"My mom's working," I say. She'll be inside at the

lodge's front desk, waiting for the parking lot to empty out before she comes down to the lake. "I'm not sure if my dad will make it. He said he'll try, but he might have to cover someone's shift."

Dad works three hours away in Bryce, just like half the people in this town. He's a ranger with the national park—so was Luce's dad, until they fired him last spring—and he's home so rarely that I don't always recognize his truck in the driveway.

"Well," Mrs. Bristow says, "tell your mom to take two candles. She can light one for him if he's running late."

"I'm sure she will." I smile, aiming for reassuring. "Don't worry. Everything's gonna be great. They'll love it."

For a moment we lock eyes, and I know neither of us is sure exactly who I mean. Her mouth opens, a question, maybe, taking shape, but a volunteer calls to her, waving her over.

"I'm sorry, Nan. If you'll excuse us?"

I barely have time to nod before she and Mr. Bristow are heading for the lot entrance. A group of volunteers parts to let them pass. Silence carried with them, but it only lasts a moment before the noise starts up again. People everywhere, checking lists, carrying boxes, and all the while, wearing those damn T-shirts. No matter where I turn, there they are—Edie, Luce, and Jane. Their awful, empty smiles.

I look down at the T-shirt Mrs. Bristow gave me. I should duck into the lodge bathroom and slip it on. Leave the shirt I'm wearing in my mom's staff locker, go down to the beach dressed like everyone else. Light my candle and send my little paper boat out onto the water.

But I can't. When I got up this morning, there wasn't any choice. I put on cutoffs, sandals, and one of my dad's old button-ups hanging open over my bathing suit. Just like what I was wearing the day the girls disappeared, to make sure they recognize me when I go to say goodbye.

I drop the shirt in a box of spares on my way out of the parking lot. Back out to the road, the lake spread below. Already the shore is thick with onlookers. I can hear music playing, faint on the wind. Jane's favorite song. I remember she sang it that day, in the canyon. Stood there by the water's edge with her eyes closed as her voice echoed off the stone. If I went back, would I hear it still? Would I find them all there waiting for me?

Is that what you want? a voice like Luce's whispers in my head.

I lift my chin, let the wind slice across my neck. Of course, I tell her. I miss you. I love you all so much.

She laughs, low and long, and as I start down toward the lake, I hear her answer. Yeah, right, she says. Yeah fucking right.

NOW

The vigil should have started by now. It's been an hour since I arrived at the lake's edge, since a volunteer herded me up onto the deck at Bullfrog's and left me to wait with all the other VIPs. That's what we are, really. That's what this is. A fucking luxury box for family and friends, set apart from the rest of the crowd that's jockeying on the beach for the best view. I lean against the deck railing, try to count the people gathered below. It's more than I've ever seen in Saltcedar before, and that's not including everyone watching from the boats dotted across the lake. They've been out there since the sun came up. Swimming, Jet Skiing. Having a perfect summer day before dropping anchor for the night's entertainment.

I check behind me, searching for the Bristows or the Gales. Nothing yet. They're probably still waiting inside the restaurant. Bullfrog's dining room is cramped and the whole place smells like stale beer, from its uneven floor to the life preservers hanging on the walls. But at least it's private. Quiet too. If only they'd invited me to join them.

Instead I'm out here listening to the crowd, to plastic scraping across the deck as a volunteer sets up rows of white folding chairs. To the feedback shriek from the microphone as someone plugs it in. I won't be using it. I won't be standing up there, telling everyone about my best friends. They didn't ask me to speak—

No, they asked me not to speak. What were they afraid they'd hear?

"Nan? Has anyone seen Nan?"

I turn in time to see my dad cutting across the deck. Tall, broad shouldered, and still wearing his park ranger uniform. He must've sped the whole way from Bryce to make it in time.

"Dad," I call. "Over here."

His eyes find mine, and he smiles. Too wide to be appropriate, but nobody will care. Everybody loves Don Carver.

"Hey, sweetheart," he says, joining me at the deck railing. "There you are."

He gives me a hug. I go loose, let his body hold mine up. Mom's been busy at the lodge all day, and I don't mind being alone—I can handle myself—but it's a relief to see him all the same.

"Hi," I say. My arms tight around his waist, his badge digging into my cheek. "I'm really glad you're here."

"I said I would be, didn't I?"

Yeah, but that's never meant much. Especially not this past year.

I pull away. Will myself to stand tall. "How'd you make it in time?"

"One of the officers coming down escorted me. Put on his lights and told me to stay behind him." Dad laughs. "I think we did about ninety-five the whole way." He shakes his head, staring past me to the lake beyond. "God, this is something, huh?"

He keeps talking, but I'm not listening. One of the officers coming down, he said. Down here? To Saltcedar?

The police haven't had much presence in town since they called off the search. A February press conference, the old sheriff working hard not to say what most people had decided was the truth by then—that if the canyon hadn't killed them that summer, the winter certainly had. After that, the cruisers stopped parking at the foot of my driveway. I slept through the night without police lights waking me up. And then Sheriff Perris retired, and the new sheriff took office, and I figured it was as over as it was ever going to be.

But sure enough, now that I know to look for them, I can spot at least two police boats out on the lake, bobbing side by side. Glistening white hulls, each one marked by a pair of small blue flags.

What the fuck are they doing here? More questions, more poking and prying. They're no better than the reporters, rats picking through the leftovers of my girls and their lives. Didn't they get what they needed last summer? I told them the truth. As much of it as they have a right to, anyway.

Anger simmers behind my ribs, but I tamp it down. Step back from the deck railing so abruptly that Dad raises his eyebrows.

"Sorry," I say. "I just . . . I think I need a minute."

His smile falls. His sympathy is too soft; it sets a phantom itch across my skin. "You know I'm happy to hang out with you. We can talk about whatever you want."

"Actually, do you mind checking on Mom?" I dig my nails into my palm. "I've barely seen her all day, and I think she was supposed to help with the families."

"The families?"

"Just the Bristows and the Gales," I say before Dad can get started on Mr. Allard. He won't be as nice about it as Mrs. Bristow was. "Please? She might be inside."

"Sure," Dad says after a moment. "I'll check. See you in a minute."

He squeezes my hand and heads toward the door. He

probably won't find Mom there, but he might be able to tell me what the holdup is with the vigil. Has one of the parents broken down? Or are they arguing about the program? Fighting over who'll read what poem in what order, as if what they say matters? We know by now how it'll play out. We know whose pictures the news will show when they mention us at the bottom of the hour. Always Jane, sometimes Edie. Almost never Luce—nobody can find a shot of her smiling. And when they need to fill time, they'll play that clip someone got of me on the lakeshore last year, a foil blanket wrapped around my shoulders while I stand there looking like shit.

I wonder what they'll get of me this year. I practiced for it. Learned how not to smile for the news crews and their cameras. How to keep from staring at the people in the crowd pointing their phones in my direction, blocking their own eyes from view.

What if it isn't enough? What if I can't give them what they're after?

I bite down hard on the inside of my cheek. Let the flash of pain pull me back, bring me home to my body. Everything will be fine, Nan. Everything will be just fine.

At last the sun slips behind the canyon ridge across the lake. A crystal hush over the crowd as I sit between my parents, three rows back from the microphone. All of us waiting, hanging motionless in that last, luminous blue hour before dark. If it were any other summer, I'd be calling Edie, saying, "Let's go for a ride." Edie and me and the bike she stripped the brakes off, just to see if she could.

Some things you have to give up.

Mom rests her hand on my leg, her fingertips digging into my thigh. "You okay?"

I nod. "Are they starting soon?" I've been dreading this for weeks. The faster we're through it, the better.

"Just a minute. See?"

She nods toward the door leading off the deck where the Bristows are huddled shoulder to shoulder with a man I don't recognize. He must be someone they know from Salt Lake, which makes me hate him a little, the same way I hate all of Jane's friends from home. They hoarded so much of her. Winters and birthdays and early school mornings. Meanwhile, here in Saltcedar, we'd have traded half our lives away to have her for the rest of them.

I face forward again. Slouch against Mom, my arms folded across my chest. "Why did they have us sit down if they weren't ready?"

"Try to relax. It's only a little delay." She kisses the crown of my head. "At least this way your dad and I could both make it in time, right?"

Is that relief I hear, or something bitter? I'm not sure.

She was one of the last to come down from the lodge, and I could tell by the flush of her cheeks as she burst onto the deck that she'd hurried the whole way. Afraid, I think, that I would have to do this all alone. Except there was Dad standing next to me.

"I'm so glad you're here," she told him as he hugged her. And then, pitched low enough that I know I wasn't meant to hear it, "You could've called."

A stir of movement draws my attention. The Bristows are coming to take their seats, led by a volunteer. The Gales trail after them, Edie's mom clinging to a mascara-blackened tissue.

"Here we go," Mom says. "Don?" She reaches across me. Tugs on Dad's sleeve. "Don, they're about to start."

Dad's been twisted around talking to someone in the row behind us, the two of them chatting like they're at someone's retirement party and not the closest thing we've had so far to a funeral for my best friends. Now he sits back, looking embarrassed.

"Sorry," he says. "Oh, are we in the wrong row? Should we move up?"

With the Bristows and the Gales settled into their seats, it's clear that they've left the row in front of ours empty.

Mom shakes her head. "It's for the Allards," she whispers. Like it's supposed to be kept secret. "In case Kent shows up, or . . ."

Or Luce's mom. Maggie Allard, who's somewhere on the East Coast, according to the goodbye letter she left behind. Finally free of this town the way Luce dreamed of being all her life. If she didn't come back to help with the search for her daughter last summer, why the hell would she come back for this?

It's funny—I never used to think she had the right idea leaving, but today I wish I'd followed in her footsteps. Wherever she is, it must be better than this.

I grit my teeth, gather every piece of myself until I'm pressed down to diamond, to pure will. In a few hours the vigil will be over. I can get through anything; I can do whatever I have to.

Up at the front of the deck, the head volunteer takes the microphone and switches it on. Everyone sits up straighter. It's time.

"Thank you so much, everybody, for coming," the volunteer says. I half expect a cheer from the crowd, but then, this isn't the Saltcedar I know, loud music on the lakeshore and fireworks set off by someone too young to be that drunk. "I'll turn it over to the families in just a minute, but before we begin, we'll have a moment of silence in honor of the girls."

Around me, people bow their heads and clasp their hands. Silence, the volunteer said, but I know for almost everyone here it will be prayer too. I get it. I've done the same thing. Knelt by the edge of my bed, waited for a voice to thunder down from the sky. But the girls were all I ever heard.

Wind buffets the microphone, its whistle carrying from the speakers on the deck until a volunteer remembers to turn the volume down. Behind me, someone's stomach growls. I almost burst out laughing. This is just so ridiculous. All of us gathered here wearing our most solemn faces, when really Luce hated Bullfrog's after they didn't hire her for that job bussing tables. Jane refused to swim at this beach—she said it smelled like motor oil and rotten leftovers. And Edie would've died all over again before she let them use that picture they've plastered everywhere.

"Nan." Mom draws me in close, our heads bent together. "Deep breath, honey. You're getting a little worked up."

Worked up? No, I am not worked up; I'm out of my fucking mind. We all should be. To mourn them like this, to wish last summer back to life when it was such a mess to begin with? It's a knife in the back, a betrayal too big for me to hold with both hands.

So I won't try. I sag against Mom. Shut my eyes, count to ten, but it doesn't do any good. Even in the dark I can still see us. Single file, climbing up one of the slots that branch off the main canyon passage. Black desert varnish striped across the red rock walls, and that ring of white high above our heads, left there when the water levels dropped.

Did the girls know what would happen to them that day? Did they see it coming somehow?

A shout from out on the water, loud enough that Mom gives a little hum of disapproval. I sink farther into her arms. Probably some tourist who came to gawk at the dead girls.

But then there's another. And another, and the rumble of an engine starting up. The speakers crackle as Mrs. Bristow turns the volume back up. "Please try to be quiet," she says into the microphone, her voice thick with tears. "It's only a moment we're asking for."

Somebody calls back in response. Too far away for me to understand and half drowned out by another engine sputtering to life, but I can hear the urgency in it. The panic.

"What is it?" I say. Mom's arm goes tight around me. I shrug it off and get to my feet. "What's going on?"

No one answers. The nearest volunteer is already making a phone call, and the others just stare at me, open-mouthed, as I push past my dad. Mrs. Bristow has backed away from the deck rail to talk to the Gales, giving me a path past her. I take it. Squeeze between two Bristow family friends and in front of the microphone until the deck rail is pressed to my ribs. From here I can see what broke the moment of silence: one of the police boats is moving out on the lake, cutting left into open water.

I squint into the distance. Follow the line they've taken, until—there. A dark spot bobbing in the water.

My breath catches. A chill, a shiver as the hairs on my arms stand up. What is that? Somebody's outboard motor, or a drink cooler fallen overboard. But nothing like that would've required the police. None of that would've brought the vigil to a halt.

"Let's sit down," Mom says, coming up behind me. "I'm sure it's nothing."

I don't think so. Not when the second police boat is moving too. Mrs. Bristow, the volunteers, their faces ashen and their eyes wide—I've seen all this before, haven't I? Which means there's only one thing it could be out there. A body.

"No," I say. "No, that can't be right."

"Nan, please. You shouldn't look."

Mom keeps talking, but all of me is there in that first police boat, bent low over the side as it eases closer and closer to the shape in the water. Which of my girls is it? And what's left of her? Will there be enough to bury?

The boat reaches the body. Two figures emerge from under the hardtop.

"Okay," Mom says. "That's enough." She grabs my

shoulder. Angles me away so I can't see anything else, and at her touch, my will breaks. The fight in me gone like a candle blown out.

She leads me back to my chair and sits me down. Heart hammering, legs trembling. I want to look for the Bristows, the Gales—I want to know how they're taking it, see which of them has dissolved into tears—but I can barely see past my own knees.

"Is this happening?" I say. "Is it actually happening?"

Mom's crouched in front of me. Her face is creased with worry as it ripples into view. "We don't know anything, okay? There's something in the water. That's all."

"Who is it? Which one?"

"We can't even be sure it's a person, honey."

"It has to be." Fear creeps up the back of my neck, cold and clutching. This isn't how it was supposed to go.

"Excuse me," I hear someone call out. When I look up, a volunteer has her hand raised. A phone held to her ear, her eyes wide. "I have it."

Everyone on the boat is watching her. The parents, the other volunteers. We know what's coming. I think of Edie and Jane, running ahead of me into the dark. Edie and Jane, waiting for their turn to rest.

"Okay, it's secondhand, so I don't—"

"Fucking spit it out," Mr. Bristow says. I've never heard him swear before.

The volunteer clears her throat. "They think it's Luce Allard. They want to know if her family's here."

Someone lets out a muffled sob. Disappointment rushes through me, an emptiness behind it. If I had to see any of them again—if the canyon only gave back one body to bury—

"Wait, hold on," the volunteer says as people start to interrupt. She's still got her phone to her ear. "Just a second. I think there's something else." The air drum-tight as she listens. Finally, she starts to smile. "They're saying she's alive. Luce is alive."

It slips into me like a needle. Alive. She said alive. They pulled a body from the water, but it wasn't a body. It was a person.

"Nan," Mom says, smiling. "Honey, did you hear that?"

No, I didn't. Somebody else is at work in my muscles, my bones, while I slip beneath the surface—crumble to ashes—harden to stone. This is impossible. Luce is dead. The girls are all dead. And I should know, because I'm the one who killed them.

NOW

They deserved it, but I can't say that. And as much as I loved them, I'm happy they're gone. I can't say that either.

Luce first, in the canyon cut. A rock in my hand and her back to me. The quick crack of her skull. And then Edie and Jane deep in Devil's Eye, our favorite swimming hole, both of them lured into the current to drown.

One, two, three. Hat trick. Clean sweep.

I have to remind myself sometimes that that's how it really happened. If I don't, the story I told the police takes root. Blooms between me and the truth until it's all I know—the four of us in a little boat, heading for the canyon on a summer evening, just like always. Only that night we made a mistake, set off with no mooring rope and no anchor, which meant one of us had to stay behind to keep the boat from drifting. So I did. The girls told me where they were going. They told me they'd only be gone a few hours. Then they followed the trail through the canyon arch, and they never came back again.

That's what I see when I dream about that day. Not the blood under my fingernails. Not Edie's hair catching in the current. Just me in that little boat, waiting and waiting until the sun burns out.

Hushed conversation and the flash of police lights through fogged glass. Mrs. Gale weeping into her husband's shoulder, Mr. Bristow with his head in his hands. It's last year all over again, only this time I'm not lying when I say I don't know what the hell's going on.

The police haven't let any of us leave—just funneled us off the deck and into Bullfrog's, told us to sit tight and keep away from the windows. One of the officers stayed behind to guard the restaurant's front door while the remaining three or four went back out to the beach. Wrangling the crowd, taking statements. Processing every single person who came to the vigil while the rest of us wait for answers.

I think we'll be waiting awhile. The officers here are stretched thin, and it'll be another couple hours before any others arrive. They're coming down from Bryce, along with the sheriff, plus an ambulance for Luce.

No, I tell myself, not Luce. Not really, because she's dead. I remember how she dropped. Blood beading on the desert dust. I checked her pulse and felt nothing. I waited ages for her to breathe and she never moved a muscle.

So whoever pulled this girl out of the water must've fucked up on a massive scale, and as soon as they let me in the room with her, I'll prove it to them. I'll show them a liar, or someone playing a joke. A tourist kid obsessed with those poor missing girls who didn't think it would be that big of a deal. After all, it's only Luce, right? The one they almost never showed on TV. The one who wouldn't have anybody waiting for her to come back.

They were wrong about that. Mr. Allard might have skipped the vigil but he's here now, escorted in by one of the officers about half an hour ago. He didn't say a word to anyone. Just took a seat at the bar, looking stiff in a white button-down, his hair combed and parted. Dressed like that, I think he must have meant to come to the vigil at some point. Why didn't he ever show?

Likely because he knew he wasn't welcome. Most of the locals are sick of seeing him passed out at the end of the bar, and he's not exactly a favorite with the Bryce County

Sheriff's Department either—he never shook their suspicion after his wife skipped town. I'd bet anything that's why they're making him wait here with us instead of taking him to the girl, wherever they've got her.

Say something, I want to call out to him. Demand to go see her. Make them prove to you it's really Luce so we can all end this farce and go home.

For a moment his gaze swings away from the other parents and over to me, where I'm tucked into a booth along the side wall. Our eyes meet—I flush hard, stare at my shoes. I forgot, I think, that he could see me too.

I've lived across from the Allards my whole life. I've watched through my windows as they argued, ate dinner, fell asleep in front of the television. I saw their lives take shape, and when Luce's mom left, I saw them fall apart the same way. All that spring, the trash piling up by the bins, Luce's light on late into the night.

It's only gotten worse after last summer. Since the girls disappeared, he's been haunting that house. Coming out only to drink himself dead at the bar, to tell stories and lies.

She's alive, he says to anyone who will listen. I saw her once, out there in the dark. She was my Lucy and she was looking for a way to come home.

The whole town's always called it bullshit. Maybe after today people will change their minds, but I won't.

"I think you should ask to speak to her," Mr. Gale says to the Bristows. They're gathered at one of the larger tables in the restaurant, sitting so politely that you'd almost think they were waiting for someone to take their order. "We deserve to know what's going on. She could know where Edie is. Or Jane. Both of them."

Everybody knows better this time, don't they? Last summer it took weeks for the Gales to let the Bristows lead the charge, but they've learned what deep pockets and Salt Lake influence can do.

"We already asked," Mrs. Bristow says. For a moment I imagine telling her the truth. Whispering it into her ear, watching her eyes go wide. Hearing her breath catch in the space behind her heart. "They said to wait, Mark. The best way to get them to talk to us is to cooperate."

I don't know if she's right, but I do know we won't hear a word until the sheriff gets here. The police were easier to win over last year and they paid the price, had half their shit leaked to the press. They know better now too.

Dad's been sitting with the other parents but he steps away. Drops onto the vinyl-covered bench next to me, forcing me to shift closer to the wall. It's just the two of us here; the police sent Mom up to the lodge to help organize a command center there pretty much as soon as they could.

"Well," he says, nudging my shoulder with his, "what

do you think? Is anybody ever gonna swim in that lake again?"

"Why wouldn't they? They did after last summer."

"Yeah, I guess they did."

And if they ever stop coming, the tourists with their RVs and their speedboats, Saltcedar is fucked. This town lives and dies by the water; it didn't even exist until they dammed the river some thirty years back, flooded most of the canyon. Made a lake so blue it was cut from a dream, so clear that even from the launch ramp you can see the markers on the bottom some government scientist left behind to track the water levels. People have been coming here ever since, shacks and lean-tos cropping up along the shore each summer until some developer saw an opportunity and took it.

What would happen if it all stopped? The lodge would close. Mom's job would disappear. We'd have to go to Bryce with Dad, hold our breath while she looked for more work. I don't know if we'd ever make ends meet again.

"It's gonna be okay, right?" I ask Dad suddenly. He jumps, looks over at me like he forgot I was there.

"What?"

"Nothing. Never mind."

"Okay, kiddo." He nods to the front door. "You all right if I go check in out there? I think that's Officer Notch at the door."

I'd rather be alone anyway. "Sure."

"Did you ever meet him? I can't remember. He does this great impression of—"

"It's fine, Dad. Go ahead."

He kisses my forehead and gets up. "I'll be right back."

He won't, I think, watching him cross the room. Once he's done with Officer Notch, he'll just find someone else to talk to. That's Dad. Everywhere we go, there's someone he knows. He's on a first name basis with half the police after last summer, and the other half he already knew from Bryce, where the rangers and the cops are so closely linked that they run a joint basketball team.

I've never understood it, that easiness with people. Edie and Jane had it, and even Luce had her moments. But the easiest part of anyone for me is the moment after they're gone.

Was it like that at all for Mr. Allard? Was he secretly relieved, to lose both of his girls? And is he terrified now at the possibility, however remote, however ridiculous, that one of them is back?

I glance over at him, eager to search for some scrap of that fear in his silhouette, only to find that he's looking in my direction again. This time I don't shy away. Everyone else here sitting around that same table together while the two of us watch.

I know you, I think.

As if he hears me, he stumbles to his feet. Reaches for something behind the bar, and then he's coming over, a bottle held by his side.

I'll ask him. If he sits down, I'll ask him the question I've only barely managed to hold back since we heard the news: Do you believe this? Or do you see it for the bullshit it is?

But he doesn't sit. Instead he stops an arm's length away from the booth and holds the bottle out to me. "Here," he says. "Water."

I stare at him, hands folded in my lap. Surprise keeping me still—surprise and maybe something else. I'm not sure.

After a moment, Mr. Allard sets the bottle down on the table. "Well, it's there. If you want it." Another pause before the rest comes tumbling out, low and gruff: "Your father shouldn't be leaving you alone like that."

I raise my eyebrows. They just told him they found his long-lost daughter, and this is what he cares about?

"I'm fine." I push the water bottle back toward him, until it's at the table's edge. "But thanks for your concern."

Mr. Allard sighs. "Okay, Nan," he says, and steps away. Back to his seat at the bar, to waiting for news that's probably hours off.

And it should be easy to dismiss. It's just Mr. Allard, just a handful of nothing on a day filled with so much.

But I keep hearing it in the space between one second and the next. Your father shouldn't be leaving you alone like that—as if I need protecting. As if the danger's out there in the world and not here in my body, sleeping in my bed and smiling with my mouth.

None of these people ever notice her, the Nan I know from last summer. She was everywhere then, reflected in every mirror. Watching me from my bedroom vanity, from the rearview in my mother's car. From the water's surface in Devil's Eye as I peered into the deep. She seemed older than me, sometimes. Angrier. Like she had her reasons and I had mine.

She's been a stranger lately, my mirror-girl, left me to do it all alone. But she comes to me now. Reaches up with her long, thin fingers and shuts my eyes. It'll be all right, she says. I promise.

THEN

Twenty bucks for a morning's work. It's not much but I took it, threw on one of Mom's spare uniform polos and walked down from our house with her in the faint blush of dawn to stand here at the lodge's front desk. Checking people in, showing first-time visitors the best beaches to swim at, and all the while wondering what the girls are doing without me.

According to the clock, it's nearing midday, so they're probably all awake by now. Jane getting dressed in her suite upstairs. Edie in her bedroom back in the prefabs, or more likely already over at Luce's house. She's been hanging out there a lot since everything with Luce's mom this spring. Just the two of them—long bike rides after school, sleepovers, even a weekend trip to Bryce I only learned about after the fact—and I've smiled and let it happen like that, because I know if I said anything, Edie would turn it around on me.

The desk phone rings. I jump and move to answer it, but Mom bats me out of the way. She hates when I take these half-shifts. Shoulders whatever work she can, averts her eyes when her boss slips me my pay in cash.

"You shouldn't have to," she'll tell me on the walk home. As if saying that is enough to change the number in our bank account. Well, shit costs what it costs, Mom. We are where we are.

She picks up the receiver, her customer service smile fixed in place. "Saltcedar Lodge, front desk. Can I help you?" A pause as she listens, and then her smile relaxes into something genuine. It must be a local calling. "Hi, Luce."

"That's Luce?" I lean across Mom to get a look at the screen on the phone's base, where the room number is displayed if the call's coming from a lodge phone. Room 200. That's the Bristows' suite. "She's here already?"

"Yes, of course," Mom says into the receiver. "We'll send some up right away." A click as she hangs up. "Nan, really? You almost knocked me over."

"Sorry."

She shakes her head, smiling. "It's fine. Will you run

some towels up to the suite? Luce said two or three. The full-sized ones, okay? Not washcloths."

"Got it," I say, coming around the front of the desk. "Can I take my break once I'm done?"

"Sure. I need you back right after, though. We've got a bunch of checkouts at noon."

"Okay. See you in a bit."

"I mean it, Nan," she calls after me, but I'm already across the lobby and heading for the laundry room. If Luce is here with Jane, Edie probably is, too, which means my break is ten minutes I can spend with the three of them.

It won't be enough. It never is. But my girls are the light off the water. They're heaven and high summer, they're clasped hands in the dark, and I'll take whatever I can get.

The elevator lets me out on the second floor. I tuck the stack of towels under my arm and head down the hallway, toward the Bristows' suite. Without the view of the lake as a distraction, it's hard not to count all the cracks in the paint, the threadbare patches in the carpet. None of it will ever get fixed; these days the lodge spends its money on its fleet of houseboats or on making its nicest rooms even nicer. They even put another TV in the suite after Jane mentioned wanting one for her bedroom.

I can hear her now through the gap where the suite door has been left ajar, telling some story about one of her Salt Lake friends while Edie laughs. Nothing from Luce, but I know she's there, listening with that blank look on her face that makes you want to impress her.

If I weren't working, I'd just go straight in, but I stop at the door, knock twice the way my mom said to. "It's Nan."

"Come in," Edie says. "It's open."

Inside, the air is gauzy with sun, sweet with the smell of fresh shampoo. A room service tray rests on the coffee table, and an old sitcom plays, muted, on the TV. There's Luce stretched out on the couch. Edie cross-legged on the floor in front of it, her head tipped back against Luce's hip, and Jane sitting opposite, her hair wet from the shower. Through the window beyond, the canyon, red as cherries, and the lake beacon-bright.

Something in me settles, a deep, silent sigh. At last, everything exactly where it should be.

Well, almost. Looking at them, tangled together in a perfect little knot, it's obvious—the three of them were here overnight. Without me.

A pang of envy hits me hard, but it fades as soon as I remind myself that I'd have had to bail regardless. My dad's back from Bryce for a few days, and my mom likes me home when he's here. They all knew I wouldn't be free. Besides, we only have two more weeks before Jane goes back to Salt Lake. I can't really blame them for making the most of it.

Jane twists around, her grin widening when she sees me. Perfect, white teeth, the kind you have to pay for. "Hey! You brought the towels?"

"Yeah." I hold up the stack. "Should I put them in your bathroom?"

She gets to her feet. "That's okay. I can take them."

"Thanks."

I catch a breath of her perfume as she carries the towels into her room. Apples and blackberry, the same one she wears every summer. It suits her. Sweet without sugar and green like spring. When Jane smiles, you know she means it.

Not Edie. She's trickier to solve, but that only makes me want to try harder. To get closer—to undo her—to lay my hands on her even now as she sits there on the floor, long dark hair and quicksilver eyes.

"Did Jane flood the shower or something?" I say, teasing. Look at me, Edie. I'll say anything, do anything, as long as you're looking.

She tilts her head. "What?"

"The extra towels."

"Oh! No, we just didn't have enough."

Quiet, for a moment. Her focus shifts to Luce; I feel it like a fire going out.

"It should be a good lake day," I say, louder so that Jane can hear. Maybe she can help pull Edie back to me. "You guys want to go later?"

"Later when?" Jane calls before coming back into the suite's main room. She drops down onto the couch. Jostles Edie, who flicks the ball of her ankle hard, earning herself an absent-minded shove from Luce. "Like tonight?"

"Like in an hour or two. I should be off work by then." Too much later and I'll have to miss it again to be home for dinner.

Jane doesn't answer, looking to Luce instead, who just shrugs. While she's obviously listening, she hasn't acknowledged me once, or even looked up from her phone. She does this with us sometimes. Goes silent and sullen, disappears without leaving. I used to take it personally, but I know her too well for that by now.

"Maybe," Jane fills in when Luce says nothing. "Provided Edie doesn't take the whole afternoon getting dressed."

Edie frowns. "Choosing a bathing suit is an art."

"Exactly," I say. "And you can't rush art."

A beep from the front door of the suite, a click as it unlocks. I look behind me in time to see a woman come bustling in. Jane's mother, wearing a crisp white shirt and a pair of floral shorts I've heard Jane call hideous.

"You girls are still inside?" she says as she digs through

one of the beach bags dangling from the coatrack. "It's a beautiful day. You should be out there getting some sun."

"In a little," Jane says. "What are you looking for?"

"Your father forgot his suit. We're taking the boat out if you want to come." Empty-handed, Mrs. Bristow heads for her bedroom door. Flashes me a smile as she passes. "Nan! There you are. How are you, honey?"

"I'm good."

"Your mom and dad are doing well, I hope?"

"For sure." It's not a real answer, but it wasn't a real question either. And the mention of my mom reminds me that she's at the front desk, waiting for me to come back. As much as I'd like to stick around, go with the girls on the Bristows' boat, my break will have to wait. "Actually, I'm still on the clock, so I should go check in with her."

Mrs. Bristow nods. "Tell her hello for me."

"Of course." I look to the girls. Luce is yawning while Edie stretches, the hem of her T-shirt riding up. "I'll see you later?"

"Probably, yeah," Jane says. "Thanks again for the towels."

"No problem."

With one last look at them, I slip out the suite door, Edie's voice following me as she yells, "We'll leave you a nice tip!"

NOW

When I'm all of myself again, it's hours later, in the staff room at the lodge. I was there as we were finally led up the road from the lakeshore; I was there as two uniforms guided me and Dad into the lobby and around the front desk. But it happened to someone else—to the girl in the mirror who called herself my name.

I rub the blurriness from my eyes. The futon beneath me creaks as I sit forward. Across from me, the kitchenette with its peeling gray countertops and dripping tap. In between, a lunch table, napkins shoved under one leg to keep it level. I used to do my homework in here when Mom had a shift, before I got old enough to stay home alone.

Mom. She's here in the lodge somewhere, but I haven't

seen her since she left the deck at Bullfrog's. And there's no sign of her here. Just the muffled hum of activity filtering in through the door from the lobby beyond.

The volunteers, the police, the families—they'll hate this girl so much when they realize what she is. Did she really think the charade would be worth it? Did she really think it would last?

I would know my girls by the sound of their breathing, by the weight of their footsteps on the shore. Every piece of our friendship collected, treasured, tucked away in a long pine box for safekeeping. Dressing up in matching Halloween costumes, celebrating birthdays on the deck at Bullfrog's. Racing bikes from the prefabs to the shore and seeing who was fastest. It's all there. I remember every bit of it. And this girl thinks she can get away with calling herself Luce?

Absolutely not. There is no world in which I wouldn't see her for the fraud she is.

The staff room door swings open. I rub my eyes, blink back a few stray tears as Mom hurries in. "Okay," she says, "I couldn't find a toothbrush, but I did find you another layer."

I barely lift my arms in time to catch the crewneck Mom throws my way. It's too big and smells of cologne. I wonder who she borrowed it from. Or how she knew I was cold.

We must have spoken already, already seen each other and gotten everything sorted, only I can't remember. Maybe that should frighten me—maybe it does—but I relax into it, a familiar sense of comfort settling over me. I will know what I need to. That much I can trust.

"Where's Dad?" I ask. I don't remember him leaving either.

Mom heads for the kitchenette and starts searching the cupboards, her back to me. "He's out in the lobby, I think."

Another comfort. Back to normal, just Mom and me, as if Dad's off in Bryce and this is any other day. They're the sun and the moon, my parents. They're not supposed to share the sky for very long.

I tuck my hair behind my ears, pull at a thread on the crewneck's sleeve. "What about the Bristows? The Gales?" Do not ask about her, don't, don't. But I can't help it. "The girl?"

Mom braces against the counter, bows her head. When she speaks, her voice is tight and strained. "The Gales are in one of the guest rooms upstairs, and the Bristows will be too once they're finished moving out of the suite."

"Moving out? Why?"

At last she turns around. "They're giving the suite to the police. For Luce."

I only barely managed to hold my tongue in public.

Now that it's just me and Mom, I don't bother trying. "Really?" I say. "You believe that?"

"Believe what?"

"That it's actually her."

Mom hesitates. A long, held breath as she considers her words, and then: "Who else would it be?"

"I don't know. Someone playing a prank. Or it could be just a different body."

"Just a different body?"

She looks stricken, but I wave it off and keep going. "You know what I mean. People have gotten lost in the canyon before. It could be one of them."

"Nan. Honey, they said she was alive."

Her tone rankles me. I don't need to be placated.

"I'm serious," I say. "Think about it. I mean, the girls have been gone a year. People have looked for them. Their pictures have been everywhere and nobody's found anything. And then today, on the day everybody's watching, one of them miraculously shows up?"

"You're right," Mom answers tightly. "The pictures *have* been everywhere. People know what she looks like. I think they're pretty sure it's her."

"But who's even seen her? Anyone who actually knows her?"

"Nan—"

"Her dad? Me? Or has it just been—"

"Nan!" Mom's palm cracks down on the counter. I jump. "That's enough, okay?"

My shock ebbing, but still I can only stare at her, wide-eyed. She never raises her voice. Not to me.

"I know you have questions," she says, more gently now. "I know you're confused. We are all fucking confused. But you have to take this seriously."

"I am," I insist.

"You're not. It's not a random body, Nan. It's not a prank. It's real, and you have to start to deal with this now. Your father and I will do as much as we can, but we can't help if you don't—" Her voice breaks. She presses the back of her hand to her mouth as a sob judders through her.

"Mom? Are you okay?"

"I'm fine. God, this isn't getting us anywhere." She glances back at the cupboard she left open. A row of mugs inside, all brought from home by her and the other lodge employees over the years. Abruptly, she asks, "Do you want some water?"

"What?"

"You should have some water."

She fills a mug, yanking the faucet so hard that the spray hits the front of her shirt. Hands it to me and drags one of the chairs away from the lunch table so she can sit in front of me. The two of us knee to knee. "Drink," she says. "We've had a long day."

I swear this is the only thing adults know how to do in a crisis. But I obey, suddenly aware of how many hours it's been since I last had anything in my stomach. And of how nice it is to let her carry everything, if only for a moment. We live side by side when Dad is gone. It's not often she can afford to make me the whole of her job.

"Okay," she tells me when I've finished. "I need to say a few things now. And I need you to listen to me. First, I am so, so glad that your friend is all right. I really am."

She pauses, leaves me a chance to argue again. I don't take it. There's no point right now—she's made her position pretty clear.

"And I don't like saying this," Mom continues. "I don't. But when all three of those girls were gone, it was a whole lot easier to call this thing an accident."

"What do you mean?"

"I mean you don't get lost for a year. Not even in that canyon. You don't get lost and come back like this." She shakes her head. Clasps my hands in hers, fear bright in her eyes. "Luce had to have been somewhere. Somebody must've taken her and kept her, and, Nan, you have to be so careful, okay? Promise me you'll be careful."

"About what?"

"About somebody taking you too. I know you don't think—"

"It's okay," I interrupt. "I'll be careful. I promise."

It leaves a bitter taste. I want so badly for her to know she doesn't need to be afraid for me. That there's no stranger out there, waiting and watching. There's only me.

But all I can do is lean in and let her hold on to me as tightly as she can. Her palm hot and broad against the back of my neck, as though I am very young and have been very far from home.

"You will never understand how much I love you," she says into my hair. "Oh, my girl. You'll never know."

Every secret I've kept from her, coiled tight, buried deep. Neither will you, I think.

After a moment too long, she lets go. Still watching me so closely, my every heartbeat written down. "So, what about us?" I ask, hoping it'll break her scrutiny. "Are we staying here too?"

Mom gets to her feet. "For tonight at least. They've got the parking lot blocked off to keep the press back. We'll see how long that lasts." She scrubs one hand through her hair. "I really don't know how we're supposed to get through this again."

Last year we had a cruiser parked on our block for weeks and that didn't stop reporters from knocking on our door. Mom still flinches anytime the bell rings.

"It'll be okay." They'll spot this girl for the liar she is and the whole thing will pass like a summer storm.

"Let's hope." Mom breathes deep, sets her shoulders. "All right. Enough of that. I'm going to get us something to eat, and then when your dad's back we can talk about finding you a change of clothes."

"And a toothbrush."

"And a toothbrush, yes." She kisses my forehead. Stays there for a moment, her mouth pressed to my skin, and I feel a quake run through her. "I'll be right back, okay?"

The staff room is quiet after she leaves. Beyond the door, dozens of people are talking about the girl upstairs, trading a name back and forth like it's worth something. They're welcome to it. I'll stay here where it can't touch me and I'll wait for it to fall apart. It won't be long.

Except I can picture it all too easily. The canyon's mouth opening wide—water and red rock, dark sky overhead—Luce's limp body twitching to life. And for the first time, I wonder. What if I'm wrong?

NOW

Dawn. A narrow tunnel through the canyon, walls leaning in and black water between. I'm in up to my hips. Hands pressed to the rock on either side of me, and I'm shivering, but it isn't cold.

"One," I am saying. "Two, three, four." Counting the striations in the stone. Layers and layers, centuries stacked parallel, bleached by the sun.

There are voices coming from up ahead, from somewhere I cannot see, so I follow them. Push deeper in, past the arch and into the canyon's secret heart. Plants growing down from the rim of the canyon above. Orchids, moss, maidenhair ferns. Blue sky and stars overhead.

It's hardly anything when I see it. Just a gap in the

rock, a slice of shadow on the edge of my sight. But the air around me goes silver and static as I get closer. A thrum in my veins like something's waking up. The gap splinters. Widens into an archway hung with desert roses, lit with morning sun.

I step through. The canyon folds over—turns and turns again, the wind at my back—until I'm somewhere else. A lake buried under the stone, water for miles as I sink to the bottom. The bed of it spreads wide below me, flat and unremarkable except for Luce. Lying on her front, her arms folded underneath her, her hair swept away from her face. I can see the lines in it left by the teeth of a comb.

My feet touch the ground. Silt billows up, catches in the currents to be carried away. The body is waiting for me. Not a mark on it. No bruises, no blood. Even her clothes are fresh and clean.

"Can you hear me?" I ask, kneeling next to her. "Luce?"

As if in answer, her body begins to rot, flesh sagging off the bone. Green and brown grime creeping up from her fingertips. Hanks of her hair begin to slip from her scalp. I blink and suddenly one of her T-shirt sleeves is torn, her shorts soaked in mud. I can see a wound on the back of her head. It's deep enough to have cracked her skull.

"Luce? Are you okay?"

She rolls over. Joints pulling and stretched under her mottled skin. A hole tears open down the side of her neck as she nods. "Of course I am." She struggles to sit up. I don't help her. "Oh. I've got something on my shirt."

She is covered in blood, in water, in the slick of the earth. "Yeah," I say. "You do. What happened? Where are Edie and Jane? I heard them earlier."

"They're in Devil's Eye. You haven't killed them yet." Luce leans in, like she's about to tell me a secret. Her eyes are clouded over, her nails coming free from their beds. "You haven't killed me either."

I wake with a headache.

Not the light of my bedroom but a heavy darkness. Patterned bedspread drawn up around my shoulders, the smell of unfamiliar detergent prickling the back of my throat. That's right. I'm at the lodge. Upstairs in one of the hotel rooms, where they finally moved us late last night.

I squint into the black until I can make out Mom and Dad in the other bed. Both still asleep, or pretending to be. They don't stir as I throw back the covers and tiptoe into the bathroom.

Shut the door behind me, let out my held breath. Turn on the lights and risk a look in the mirror. Nan from last summer looking back at me. My face and my body, my hand pressed against the glass so we're palm to palm.

She is cold to the touch; she cannot breathe. Like Luce after I hit her. Like Edie and Jane as they drowned. The blue sway of the Eye as I swam for the surface. Edie thrashing yards below me, her hand outstretched, air bubbles pouring from her open mouth. Jane's body had already disappeared into the deep, and Luce's was out in the canyon cut, blood seeping into the dirt, and it was still so loud. Everything they said to me, ringing in my ears even after they died, over and over and over—

I retch into the sink. Bile and spit, my stomach empty, heaving. Flush with shame as tears start to sting my eyes.

This isn't fair. It isn't supposed to hurt anymore. It isn't supposed to feel so close.

But it does, and when I peer past the story I told the police, I can see the truth of that night like it's a painting hung on a gallery wall. Look at this one, see? There we are, the four of us on the loading dock, keys to the lodge's skiff dangling from my hand, our secret place waiting for us in the canyon beyond.

Luce was the one who heard about it first. During one of her shifts volunteering with the Conservancy, that's what she said. She'd been poring over maps, labeling photographs, listening to cassette tapes someone recorded right before they dammed the river. And she kept finding references to it—to a great cave in the rock at the end of a long-forgotten trail. Lush hanging gardens, a large swimming hole with a narrow pebble beach, and overhead, a soaring, stone ceiling split down the middle to let in the sky.

Devil's Eye, they called it on those old tapes. Said the swimming hole was so deep and a siphon current at the bottom so strong that if you weren't careful, it would pull you through a gap in the earth and into hell itself. But we weren't afraid. We never were when we were together. Sneaking through the lodge lobby late at night, clothes dripping lake water. Setting off fireworks on the beach, daring Edie to catch the falling ash on her tongue as if it were snow. My girls made this town into something beautiful.

That's why I didn't understand what was happening at first.

It had been a normal day. Jane slept in late while Luce worked her shift at the gas station, and then we spent the evening at the lake for the end of summer party, waiting for it to be over so we could head for Devil's Eye. Edie and Luce bickered like they always did; Jane told me about a boy she liked back in Salt Lake.

Like I said. Normal. Until we got to the Eye, until we were flat on our backs by the water's edge, and Edie decided she hated me. I don't know why. Maybe I'd upset her somehow. Maybe she was just fucking bored. But she started saying these horrible things—calling me a spare part, a leech, as if we hadn't been best friends our whole lives—and Luce and Jane let her. They sat by and watched and said nothing.

What was I supposed to do? Just stand there and take it? Not a chance.

Out in the hallway, a door opens and closes. I force myself to breathe in deep. Rinse out the sink and splash some cold water on my face. Pull it together, Nan. After all, if it really is Luce they pulled out of the lake, she could tell them what I did. I have to get to her first, impostor or not; I have to see what kind of liar I'm dealing with.

I catch my face in the mirror again. My blond hair lank and too long, my eyes that dull, almost colorless blue.

What about me? What kind of liar am I?

When I told the police last year that I didn't know where the girls were, I meant it. The siphon could have taken their bodies anywhere. Water rushing under the rock, strange undercurrents and hidden tunnels. Flood and rise, drift and pull.

No, I never lied.

Never? my reflection says. Not even once? Not even to me?

I ignore her. Enough is enough. I have more important shit to worry about.

The thing is, it isn't that hard. Yes, there's a uniform stationed outside the door to the Bristows' suite, but I learned last summer how quickly the world lies down for you if you really will it to. Especially if you throw in a few fake tears.

"I'm sorry to bother you," I tell the policeman, sniffling. "I know it's not allowed. But I really thought she was dead." I dry my cheeks on the sleeve of my sweatshirt. "Please. Can I go in and visit Luce?"

He was already on edge before he ever saw me. I could tell from down the hall, could find it in the shift of his body from foot to foot. Now he clears his throat, avoiding eye contact. "You're her, right? Don Carver's daughter?"

"Yeah, I'm Nan," I say, and he seems to relax. Thank God for my dad, honestly. "Look, I really am sorry. I'm not trying to get you in trouble. And I don't even need to talk to her. If I could just see her . . ."

The policeman sighs. Runs his thumb over the radio clipped to his belt. "No promises," he says, "but I'll ask."

Fuck. I was hoping nobody else had to know. "Oh, you don't have to—"

"If it's okay with Mr. Allard, you can have a few minutes. Just to see her, all right?"

He knocks on the door before I can say a word, leaving

me to stand there with my tears all dried up and my mouth open in surprise. Mr. Allard? Does that mean they've confirmed it's her? I mean, a father always knows, right?

I force my body to relax. Fathers, but not Mr. Allard. He couldn't have picked Luce out of a lineup during those last couple months. He was too busy looking for his wife, combing through her belongings and reading online forums full of other spouses who'd been left behind.

He made a few posts of his own too. I know that because Luce found them one day. The school library during our free block, me playing lookout while she used the librarian's computer to print off page after page. She stapled them and tucked them into her backpack; the next time I saw them, they'd been highlighted and marked up like she used to do with her history notes.

At last, after a long, uncomfortable quiet, the door opens. Mr. Allard stands on the other side, one hand braced on the frame. Circles under his eyes, still dressed in yesterday's clothes.

"Good morning, Officer," he says. "What's— Oh. Nan." My name seems to float there between us, and then, as if he can't think of anything else, he adds: "You're up early."

"I hope I didn't wake you, sir," the policeman says.

Mr. Allard doesn't look away from me as he answers. "Not at all. What is it?"

"She just wanted to know if she could see your daughter."

I hold still, let Mr. Allard scrutinize me. There's a kind of skepticism in him that I think has always been there, but it's more pointed today, aimed at something deep below the surface.

"I'll come in with her," the policeman hurries to add. "It'll be quick, in and—"

"Sure," Mr. Allard interrupts. He gestures to the room beyond him. "Fine. If you want."

I step into the suite, all too aware, suddenly, of how tall he is. Relief and fear in a twin rush as he shuts the door before the policeman can follow me through. Throws the dead bolt.

"Motherfuckers," he mutters, and turns away.

I mean to go with him, but the sight of the living room stops me cold. The gray couch and its matching armchairs. The television, remotes arranged just so on the media console. Everything so exactly like it was last summer that I half expect Jane's bathing suit to still be drying out on the balcony.

Mr. Allard drops onto the couch. Nods to one of the bedrooms and says, "She's in there. Don't know if she's awake, but you can go on in."

The room he's pointing to used to be Jane's. I can't

imagine lying in that bed now, but I guess it wouldn't mean anything to the girl who isn't Luce.

"How is she?" And, because it's what I'd ask if I really believed all this: "Did she tell you where's she been this whole time?"

Her dad leans back. Mouth pulled tight as he shakes his head. "Not a word. But feel free to ask her yourself. You might have better luck."

She's been stonewalling him? She probably knows she'll give herself away the second she opens her mouth.

Or it's Luce being Luce. Not shy and not reserved, but she never talked just to talk. If she had something to say, she'd wait until the right person was listening. Maybe this time that person's me.

I will never know until I see her. One second. Another. I hold my breath—come out, come out, wherever you are—and knock on Jane's door three times.

I hear a rustle inside. Somebody moving. A light turns on and the door creaks as it eases open. Curtains drawn over the windows, hiding the lake view. The queen-sized bed unmade. A magazine from the lobby splayed open on the nightstand, showing a photograph of an ornamental garden. And a girl, halfway behind the door, her cheek resting against its edge.

I could say it's her hair that convinces me, the same

swing and curl, same sunset red. Or her eyes, lake blue, or her mouth, or the shape of her face, or, or, or.

But it's none of that at all. It's the way I can feel myself waking back up. To love her, to hate her—parts of me finding use again like a sail snapping taut in a sudden wind.

I would know you anywhere, I think. Here in this hotel or out in the canyon, standing over your body, your blood under my nails. The real Luce Allard, come back from the fucking dead.

NOW

"Oh," she says, "it's you."

I can hear her breathing. I can see her shadow on the carpet, the glow off the bedside lamp lining her in amber. She's real. This is actually happening.

"It's you," I say back to her. "I can't believe you're here."

"Me neither."

A sly quirk at the corner of her mouth. This is it, isn't it? It's all coming out. She'll slam the door in my face, and ten minutes from now the police will be here, putting me in handcuffs and reading me my rights. I'll apologize as they lead me away; I won't mean it.

But then her smile widens. I watch the stretch of her skin, fascinated, dazed. "Well?" she says. "Give me a hug."

I am too stunned to move. Pinned like a butterfly in a

box as she comes in close, as her arms wrap around my ribs. For a moment her hold on me is tight enough to hurt, but it passes so quickly I think I must have imagined it, and I'm left with just the warmth of her. The beat of her heart against my chest. Alive, it says, alive. You could kill her all over again.

"Luce," I say. "I . . . You—"

"It's okay," she says. "I'm fine."

She releases me at last, steps back, and I think I can see it in her eyes: the line of us as we climbed through the canyon, pulled thin enough to break. It fucking happened. I was there.

Wasn't I there?

"I don't understand," I say. Buried underneath my words: I have watched your body go empty. I know what you look like when you're gone. "How are you back?"

"Well," she says, "I took the elevator up from the lobby." I gape at her. "Oh, you meant that?" She nods to the suite window, to the lake beyond. "Yeah, I don't really know, I guess."

She's always had a way of catching me off guard, always laughing when I'm expecting her to cry, but to be flippant now? About this? It's bullshit, and her answer is too. God, I killed you, Luce—don't you care?

"What do you mean?" I press. Bait hung on a barbed silver hook. I know I'll bleed, and still I bite down hard.

Tell me what I did to you. Tell me how I fucked it up so I can do it better next time. "What happened?"

"I told you, I—"

"Where have you been?"

"I said I don't know. As in, I don't remember."

Like the strike of a hammer, her voice ringing in the air. "You don't?" I manage. I can't have heard her right.

Luce looks over my shoulder to where her father is still slumped on the couch. Shifts her weight, her confidence faltering for the first time. "I mean, I know something happened. I saw the posters and shit in the lobby. But the last thing I remember, we were out on the lake, heading to the Eye." The smile again, only now I can tell how hard she's working to keep it in place. "So you tell me."

Disbelief drives its thorns in deep. She doesn't remember? No fucking way. When have I ever been that lucky?

But if she's lying about this, I don't understand why. Jane would do it to protect me, all forgiveness and second chances. Edie would do it just to watch me squirm. And Luce wouldn't do it at all. Once, out in the desert past our neighborhood, I watched her scare a coyote off a half-dead mourning dove. And afterward, she didn't call the Conservancy to come look after it—instead she broke its neck with her own two hands. If Luce knew what I did to her and the girls, either I'd be in cuffs or she'd have already killed me herself.

Take her at her word, then, and it makes sense. She doesn't remember. That's why she isn't scared of me. That's why she isn't angry. Twelve months have passed since the day I left three bodies in the canyon, but for Luce they didn't happen at all. She's still out there on the lake in that little boat; I'm still her best friend, and everything is still perfect.

"Nan?" she says. "Did you hear me?"

Right—she is not a photograph, not a nightmare. "Yeah, I just . . . We thought you were dead."

Luce flashes me a grin. "Sorry to disappoint. Here, come in so I can sit down."

She steps back into Jane's old room. Waves for me to follow, and I do, held fast by her complete ease. Look at her, turning her back to me as if she has nothing to be afraid of. As if nothing ever happened.

I have to match that. Forget just the way she did. All those horrible things she said—pick them out like white-thread stitches. Never mind that they're the only things holding me shut, and never mind that I didn't want this, that I haven't regretted what I did for even a second. She was dead, and now she isn't and—

God, why the hell isn't she dead? How dare she ruin everything, coming back like this?

The door clicks shut. I lean against it as opposite me, Luce sits on the bed with her legs crossed, pulls the crisp white comforter up so it covers her ankles. Her hair falls across her face; she tucks it behind her ear and I'm reminded, bitterly, that she was always the most beautiful of us. You couldn't tell with anyone else in the room, especially Edie, but alone it was so obvious. Like looking at her was something violent.

And nothing's changed. From sixteen to seventeen, dead to alive.

"Come on," she says, nodding to the bed. "Don't just stand there."

"That's okay." Head-on, I can see every pause, every fidget. I prefer it that way. "You've been through a lot. I don't want to crowd you."

Only moments later, I get my reward. Luce's left hand in her lap, thumbnail pressing hard into the pad of her little finger. If I had any doubts, they're gone now. The Luce I grew up with has a scar on her pinky, a thick line of tissue with no feeling left in it, and I've watched her just about split it open before every midterm, every presentation, every dive off the dock into shallow water. It's really her.

More important, it's really her, and she's nervous.

About what, Luce? Is it scaring you, to be so close to me? Because something really did happen that day. The billboard over town, the vigil, the press outside—it's proof that I made three girls disappear. I'm just not sure exactly how anymore.

I guess I have to ask Luce. Carefully, slowly, just like I learned from all my interviews with the old sheriff last year. Cards held close. I can't give her anything she hasn't earned.

"I'm sorry I couldn't come see you last night," I say. It's how a friend would talk, and I'm her friend until she tells me she knows otherwise. "Your memory . . . Do they know why you lost it?"

"Not exactly," she says. "It's probably something with my head, but they checked me out last night and I wasn't bleeding or anything." She checks the clock on the nightstand. "I'm supposed to go to the hospital later so they can do a real exam."

That'll be in Bryce, a few hours away. What if she changes her story while she's there? What if she suddenly remembers everything?

"You're okay, though, right?" I ask. "Your memory must be coming back to you now that you're home."

I watch her closely. Will her to say no, to laugh it away as impossible. She just stares back at me, her eyes half in shadow.

"I guess we'll see," she answers at last. "The sheriff seems to think that the exam will tell us a lot even if I can't think of anything new." Her voice takes on a deeper pitch, her posture straightening as she imitates someone: "The body remembers." Then a careless shrug. "Whatever the fuck that means."

Involuntarily, my gaze flicks over her, from the crown of her head to the jut of her knees under the duvet. I thought nothing had changed, sixteen to seventeen, but I was wrong. She's thinner. Stronger. Or perhaps it's just the feel of her, like she's been reworked in some distant forge. Wherever she's been, I don't think it's been kind to her.

Good.

"Hey," Luce says, "this is a weird question, but do you know what they did with all my stuff?" I must look confused because she adds, "Like, did my dad get rid of my clothes?"

"I think everything's still in your room." I never saw Mr. Allard hauling bags of it out to the truck, never got a call to come over and take what I wanted from her dresser. "Why?"

"I just hate wearing this." She plucks at the blue police-issue sweats she's got on. "But it's all I have. They took the clothes I had on last night. I don't know when I'll get them back."

Not for a while, I bet. Luce was found in the same outfit she disappeared in—cutoffs and a gray T-shirt that used to be her dad's—and that only makes the question of where she's been harder to answer. The police will want to keep everything for tests, photographs, evidence logs. All the shit they couldn't do last summer without a body.

Now they have more than that. Luce could tell them the whole story. She could end the world if she wanted, but we're here in Jane's room, with every question I so badly need to ask tied up in white ribbon like flowers for a gravestone. Do you really not remember? How did you survive? And where the fuck did you go for a year?

"Nan," Luce says, leaning forward, "you're being really quiet."

The shame that takes hold of me is an old thing, born from behind my ribs. Suddenly I am sitting with Luce in the cafeteria, missing the punchline while Edie laughs. I am floating on my back in the Eye, wondering why the conversation stopped as soon as I surfaced for breath.

"Sorry," I say. "I didn't—"

"It's okay. You can be quiet if you want." Luce smiles faintly. "I'm just surprised. You haven't even mentioned Edie and Jane."

"Because they're dead," I say, too flustered to think better of it. And I can tell it catches Luce oddly—her brow furrows, thumbnail pressing harder into her little finger—but my chance to explain vanishes when there's a knock at the suite's front door.

She gets to her feet. "What?" she says. "Dead like I was?"

It rings in my ears, turns my nerves electric. She can't be suggesting they're alive, can she?

No. I'm being ridiculous. Edie and Jane drowned in the Eye and I was there. I made it happen.

And still, what if I'm wrong? The day my girls died unravels in my head. The canyon crumbles to sand. The water evaporates; the sky fades white. It's enough to root me to the spot as Luce reaches past me to open the bedroom door.

"Excuse me," she says. "You're kind of in the way."

I stumble to the side, drift after her as she breezes into the living room. "I've got it," she tells her dad, who's gotten to his feet.

The knock comes again. Insistent, louder this time. Shave and a haircut. Luce knocks back—two bits—before throwing the suite door open. "Hi, Sheriff," she says to the person on the other side. "Come on in."

The figure who crosses the threshold is tall, imposing. A woman rendered in shades of desert beige: summer-tan skin, sandy-brown hair tied back in a low ponytail. Her shoulders are too broad for the cut of her sheriff's uniform, and I can see the fabric straining as she reaches up to take off her wide-brimmed hat.

"Good to see you on your feet, Luce," she says. "How are you feeling this morning?"

"Fine. I have some questions, though."

"We do too. Kent, good to see you."

Mr. Allard grunts in acknowledgment, more alert than I've seen him since his wife left town. Two of his girls gone—does he wish he'd got the other one back instead?

The sheriff turns toward Luce again. Startles visibly when she notices me lingering by the bedroom doorway. "Hi, there," she says, her voice pulled taut. "Luce, I thought we talked about visitors."

"It's not visitors," Luce answers. "It's just Nan."

"You're Nan?" she asks me. "Nan Carver? Don's daughter?"

"Yeah."

"This is Sheriff Marsden," Luce says. "She's—"

"I remember," I interrupt. "Nice to meet you."

I knew Sheriff Perris hadn't run for reelection, but I hadn't paid much attention to his successor. It didn't matter, not when Dad kept saying a new sheriff meant the old cases like the girls' would fall by the wayside. Besides, the police never gave me much to worry about before. I figured I'd get another like Perris, who assumed the girls had just got lost in the canyon before he ever talked to me. Even when he did, the first thing he asked was if I knew how to read a map.

I said no.

But this woman is Perris's opposite. Young, sharp. And

worse, local. That's Kelly Marsden standing there, and she was born and raised in this town just like I was. Her picture's hanging in the display case by the gym at school, a plaque underneath with every record she set for the swim team, and her name slapped onto some sportsmanship award. They gave it to Edie this year, to honor her, and nobody laughed even though we all know she was never a good sport in her life.

"I was going to come by your family's room next," Sheriff Marsden says, "but I'm glad to have the chance to meet you first." She sets her hat down on the console table. I notice for the first time the thick file folder in her other hand. Is that everything from last year? What I wouldn't give for a look inside.

"Likewise," I say. "Thanks for taking care of Luce."

Marsden smiles. It doesn't fit her mouth quite right. "You must be happy to have her home again."

I sneak a glance at Luce. That'll sting if she really knows what I did—or what I tried to do, I guess. But she doesn't seem bothered. She just watches, intent and a little impatient.

"I'm not sure, though," Marsden goes on, "that it's the best idea for you to be here for this. Why don't you head back to your family and we can catch up on everything this afternoon?"

After the exam in Bryce, after Luce has a chance to tell everyone a new story. But what is there to do about it now, except hope that Luce wasn't lying to me?

God, what a fucking mess.

"Okay," I say. "I'll see you guys later."

Marsden holds the suite door open for me. I step out into the hallway, but not before one last look at Luce. Her figure wrapped in pale morning, her head turned toward the view of the lake.

We could skip all of this, Luce. We could end it nice and pretty. Hold still for me, won't you? I promise I'll hit harder this time.

"Goodbye, Nan," the sheriff says, and shuts the door.

NOW

The staff room is a shitty place for an interview. Thin walls and a gap under the door even when it's shut and locked. Someone's tried to stuff it with newspaper, but I can still hear the noise from the lobby. Phones ringing, the chime of the elevator. Voices from a reporting team filming outside and their garbled echo from the TV screen by the front desk. Wheels squeaking as a group of volunteers maneuvers a row of bulletin boards into place to block the view through the lobby's glass wall.

They were part of the vigil, those boards. Arranged like a gallery in the lobby so that people could put up photos, cards, messages for the girls, except someone's out there right now taking down everything that includes Luce. Because we don't have to mourn her anymore.

"Hey," Dad says, laying his hand over mine. "Stop that."

I look down. Blood running down the side of my middle finger where I've peeled off a thick curl of skin. I lean back from the table, wipe the cut dry on the inside of my sleeve. "Sorry. I'm just anxious, I guess."

"You shouldn't be." I think he's going for reassuring, but it sounds like a scolding. "You don't have anything to worry about."

We've been waiting here for nearly half an hour now. Dad and me on one side of the rickety lunch table, waiting for the sheriff to come take her seat on the other. Just to talk, she said this morning when she stopped by our room after seeing Luce. Just to get things down officially, for our records.

Maybe Dad bought it, but I didn't. If this were just a conversation, she wouldn't have made me wait all day for it, my unease simmering to a boil while she headed for Bryce with Luce in the passenger seat. The hospital there, the police station—strange rooms and new questions. Chance after chance for Luce to dig up a memory and sell me out.

"Dad," I say without quite knowing why. "Dad, I need to talk to you."

But it's too late. Someone knocks at the door, pushes it open without a pause. Sheriff Marsden strides through, another thick file folder tucked under her arm and a uniform following a few paces behind.

"Hi, folks," she says. "Sorry to keep you waiting."

I can feel Dad looking at me, feel the moment stretch out a touch too long. Then it snaps as he slips back into his regular charm.

"No problem." He stands, offers Marsden his hand to shake. "Whatever we can do to help."

"I appreciate that."

She drops the file onto the table. It lands with a slap, and the weight of it is enough to send a shiver of fear down my spine. All those notes, all that paperwork, for this? The last sheriff hardly ever showed up with more than a legal pad and a fucking golf pencil.

"We'll be taping this," she says, "so you're aware. Standard procedure." The uniform accompanying her has knelt by the table's edge; I recognize the police-issue recorder he's setting up. That, at least, I've dealt with before. "And are you sure you wouldn't like a lawyer? I noticed you never used one during proceedings last year, and I wanted to make sure that—"

"We're fine," my dad cuts in. "Right, Nan?"

My parents argued about it a few hours ago, the two of them crowded into the bathroom like that would keep me from overhearing. "A lawyer's expensive," Dad told Mom even as she protested. "We didn't need one before, did we?" And then, after it sounded like Mom had started to cry: "I'll be there with her, Georgia. Everything will be okay."

"Right," I say, just how I'm supposed to.

"If you're sure." Marsden runs her hands over the file like she's smoothing the wrinkles out of her just-made bed. Since I saw her this morning, she's come a little undone, her sleeves rolled up and her ponytail mussed. It must have been a long day with Luce, I think, sympathetic despite myself. If anybody knows what a pain she can be, it's me.

But I can't let on, and I can't ask what I want to—did it all come back? Does she remember?—so I settle for: "How's Luce?"

Has she told you where she was? Has she told you what I did?

"Miss Allard," the sheriff answers, sighing, "is as all right as she possibly could be, given the circumstances."

"Is she here?" Dad asks.

"No. No, she'll be at the hospital for a little while longer." Marsden's focus narrows, her eyes locking onto mine. "We're obviously hopeful that your friend will start to remember what's happened to her, Nan, but until then I'm really going to need your help. Can I count on you?"

I bite my lip to keep from smiling. I've spent all day worried that Luce was lying about her amnesia, waiting until there were miles between us until she told the police the truth. But she's had a dozen opportunities by now, and she's passed up every single one. Lying or not, she's left herself a blank page; I can be the one to fill it in.

"Sure," I say. "Of course you can."

"I hope that's true." Marsden taps the file. "There are things in here that need to stay between us."

"I know. It wasn't me who leaked things last year."

She raises her eyebrows. Surprised, maybe, that I cut to the chase, but I want her to think that's just the kind of person I am. Nan would never lie to you; Nan is always so honest, so direct.

"I'm glad to hear it," Marsden says. "Okay. I guess we can get started."

First, it's time to wade through the same shit. Roll out the story I told the old sheriff last year, the story I've told anyone who ever asked. Let Marsden look at it up close. Admire it, I think as she repeats it back to me. After all, it's almost true.

Then my father's turn, but he doesn't have anything to add. He was in Bryce—he never knew the girls that well—they were good kids, though. Obviously good kids.

It's only after we've passed Marsden's tests that she opens the file in front of her. I get a glimpse of the top sheet, of the words "Presumed Dead" next to Edie's name, but she flips past it quickly, landing instead on a printout of a photograph. I recognize its subject before she's even flipped it to face us. Red hair parted cleanly, a thick scar visible on the scalp beneath. That's the back of Luce's head, right where I hit her. I have to clench my fists to keep from reaching out, running my fingertip along the line of the wound.

But Marsden does it for me. "See that?" she asks.

My mouth goes dry. It's longer than I imagined. Beautiful, too, for what it proves to me—if nothing else, I hit Luce. I left my mark.

"Are you allowed to show us this?" Dad says. One hand lifted like he's about to cover my eyes.

"Don't worry, Mr. Carver," the sheriff answers. "The Allards gave us their permission. We're doing everything aboveboard here." She looks to me, lets her voice soften. "It's a serious scar, isn't it?"

I stare at the photograph. Watch as the scar seems to open, flesh splitting and peeling back, blood welling up in the gap. Beneath, the white gleam of bone cracked black, spattered with gray pulp.

"Yeah," I say. It's just a photograph; the wound is closed again. "It looks bad."

"It was. She's lucky she survived."

A burst of laughter, blazing up my throat, but I manage to quell it. Marsden ducks to catch my eye.

"Do you know how she got it, Nan? Because Luce's dad is pretty sure it wasn't there before she disappeared, and we can't find anything in her medical history."

I could make something up, tell them Luce took a nasty fall in the canyon a few weeks before the end. But the empty stretch of her memory doesn't reach back far enough.

"No," I say. The word sticks in my throat.

"With the angle, the depth," Marsden continues, "we think someone hit her." Dad makes a pained sound; she ignores him. "So I need you to think hard, Nan. Was there anybody you saw that summer that made you uncomfortable? Anybody you didn't know who hung around a lot?"

"Um," I start, shifting in my seat. There must be somebody I can hide behind. Just in case Luce remembers, or Marsden ever decides it's time to take aim. Not a local, nobody who could call my bluff. One of the tourists? But then the only tourist I ever paid attention to was Jane. "I'm not sure."

"She's nervous," my dad says to the sheriff. He rests his hand on my shoulder without looking at me. "She doesn't want to get anyone in trouble, but this is important, right?"

"Right," Marsden says.

Dad slides his hand across my back until he's palming the nape of my neck, the tightness of his grip both uncomfortable and reassuring. He'll take care of this. "Go ahead, honey," he says to me. "It's okay. You can tell them about Kent."

"Kent?" Marsden repeats. "Kent Allard?"

I hesitate. Luce's mom is gone; can I really send her dad away too?

Yes, I can. She's the one who wouldn't stay dead. She brought this on herself.

"Things weren't great with them last summer," I say. See? How bad can this be if I don't even have to lie? "They used to argue a lot."

Marsden nods to the uniform, who pulls out a notepad and starts writing something down. "About what?"

"Her mom," I say. "Money. School. That kind of thing."

Dad lets go of me and folds his hands on the table, leaning forward like he's sharing a secret with Sheriff Marsden. "Listen, I don't think Kent's a bad guy. It's not that at all. He's just got a temper. I used to see it on shift in the park. I think his fuse got even shorter after Maggie left. And Luce . . ." He shakes his head. "She could be tough. Really tough."

I've never heard him be so specific about one of the girls before. They've always just been "Nan's friends" to him, the three of them so fused together that Dad would sometimes forget Jane didn't actually live in town. But I guess he's noticed more than I gave him credit for.

Marsden purses her lips. "Okay," she says, "okay, that's interesting. Thanks, Don."

I can tell she's holding this case up to the light, tilting it this way and that, but I can't quite figure out what story she's spotted inside. "Do you think Mr. Allard did something to Luce?"

"I think," the sheriff says gently, "that your friend was gone a year, and whether she remembers it or not, she had to be somewhere." She taps the photo of Luce's scar. "I don't think it's anywhere she wanted to be."

So her theory is the same as my mom's, then. A bad, bad man in a bunker somewhere. Do they realize how insulting that is? Three of my friends snatched up, and me left on the shelf like I wasn't worth taking.

I wait for Marsden to go on, but she stays quiet, watching me intently. Shit, I think. Did I miss a cue? It's hard, sometimes, to figure out what people expect from me. To see the board through the eyes of someone who doesn't know the game is rigged. What questions would she have, the last girl left behind? What would she want more than anything?

The rest of her friends handed back to her. Edie and Jane made into miracles, just like Luce.

"Do you think the others are still wherever Luce was?" I ask. "Could they still be alive?"

"It's possible," Marsden answers reluctantly, "but I think we need to accept the likelihood that if Jane and Edie were being held with Luce, her escape has forced their captor's hand."

I almost feel bad for the sheriff. She has no idea how ridiculous she sounds. Because she's right as far as it goes, but that's not very far, is it? There's no captor. No one took the girls. No one did a thing to them but me.

Luce, looking at me in Jane's bedroom—dead like I was, she said, dead like I was, dead, dead, dead—

What did I do wrong? How did I let this happen?

I dig my nails into my palm. No, Nan. This isn't your fucking fault. It's Luce's. She should've stayed where you put her.

"All right," Marsden says. "I can see I've upset you."

"You have?" Too late, I feel the tear that's slid down my cheek.

"You okay, honey?" Dad asks.

The sheriff stands up. Behind her, the uniform goes to open the staff room door. "Let's stop for the moment so you can get some rest. We'll have plenty more to talk about after tomorrow."

"What's tomorrow?" I ask.

"Assuming Luce is feeling well enough, we're heading

back out to the canyon to see what we can reconstruct from her memory." Marsden grins, wolfish. "She's asked for you to come along. Moral support, I think."

"That's great," Dad says. His voice sounds far away. "It'll be good for you to get back out there, Nan."

Good for me, to climb that same path. Good for me, to feel those same currents trying to drag me under again.

I haven't been to the canyon in a year. Now I have to go back, and I have to do it with the girl I killed.

NOW

Deep evening, the lodge left behind. Go home, they said. Keep the blinds drawn and your door locked tight. As if they needed to tell us twice.

Dad puts the pickup in neutral, lets the slope of the road through the prefabs carry us the last few yards to our driveway. The Allard house across the street is dark and lonely. White scraps of paper taped to the door—I know without checking that they're notes left by reporters, names and numbers in case Luce ever feels like talking. We got our share of those last year, especially after Mom's voicemail filled up.

"Don, please," she's saying now, the truck still inching forward. "I'd like to get inside before somebody sees."

"It's fine," Dad says. I think I feel him tap the brakes. "Nobody cares about us up here. The press is still down at the lodge."

"I'd rather not take that risk. Unless you'd like to be photographed?"

I know the shape of this argument from last year. Dad wanting to be out there, searching the canyon, talking to the press. On the other side, Mom, all too aware of what that would do. The questions it would inspire people to ask about me, questions that would follow me for the rest of my life.

Dad sighs, weary. Starts to turn the wheel as we approach the corner. "Of course I don't want to be photographed. But I'm not going to gun it into our driveway, Georgia, if—"

Mom undoes her seat belt. Throws open the passenger door and steps down from the truck even as it's still moving. She stumbles, catches herself on the post of our mailbox. Dad brakes so hard I pitch forward into the back of his seat.

"Come inside, Nan," she says.

We watch her head for the house, her keys in hand. No sound but the soft, steady beep of the truck's open door alert. It never happened like that last year. I don't think so, anyway.

"It's been a long day," Dad says after she's disappeared. "Give your mom some grace." And he pulls the rest of the way in with the door still open.

My room is just the way I left it. Only yesterday morning, but it feels like ages ago. That girl who woke up, dressed in last year's clothes, practiced her respectful silence in the mirror—what did she know about anything?

I step over the laundry piled up on the floor and sit down gingerly on the edge of my bed. Under me, the mattress sags, springs squeaking like they always do; still there's a strangeness to everything that I can't shake. My sheets feel like tissue paper as I crumple them in my fists. The walls around me like painted cardboard, the space so flat I think I could push the whole room over with my little finger.

A stage—bright lights and an audience before me, Edie and Jane in the front row—Luce, waiting in the wings, a red-stained rock in her left hand—

"I'm here," I whisper. The air vibrates with it. "I know that I'm here."

I know, too, that Mom is in her bedroom. She left the door ajar; I looked in on my way past. Made sure she hadn't run off, because if Luce's mother could, why not mine?

And I know that Dad is in the kitchen. I can hear the

sink running. He's washing yesterday's dishes. If everything had gone the way it was meant to, we'd have come home from the vigil last night and had dinner together. The three of us at the table, eating in silence and doing our best not to look out the window at the Allard house.

My stomach turns at the thought. Sick with wishing, I think, but then that doesn't seem quite right.

The water shuts off. Heavy footsteps as my father comes down the hall. I lie back on the bed, draw the sheets up over my head. I'm not hiding. What's there to hide from?

"Georgia?" I hear him say. "Can I come in?"

I envied Jane. I can admit that. For her money and her nice things, sure, for her private school and her brand-new phone, but mostly for the image I'd conjured of her bedroom. The top floor of that big house in Salt Lake, far enough from her parents' room that she never heard them fight.

Murmurs from down the hall, louder with every passing second. I roll over, press my face into my pillow. Spotlight flaring—Luce makes her entrance as the audience claps—Edie and Jane throw flowers onto the stage, bouquets of orchids, all cut from the Eye—

"I said I don't want to talk about this." Mom's voice rips through the quiet. I start to hold my breath.

"We have to, Georgia. We can't just pretend—"

"Oh, one of us is pretending, but it's not me."

They're moving now, heading for the front room. If I wanted to, I could climb out my bedroom window, the way I used to last summer. Wander to the edge of the prefabs, to where a handful of lots are left empty or unfinished. I kissed Edie there once, right before it all ended. The two of us in a half-built house, sitting at the top of a staircase to nowhere. Would I find her there if I went back? Is it her turn to come home?

"It's not going away," Dad is saying. "You understand that, right?"

"Are you kidding me? I'm the one who handled it last year while you were off doing God knows what."

"Oh, come on, Georgia. I was working." I hear Mom scoff, but Dad won't have it. "I was earning us money, which we fucking need, okay?"

"Then where is it?"

No answer from Dad, but I can picture him pacing away, shaking his head. What is Mom doing, going so hard at him? He's barely ever home. Just let him rest.

"I mean it," she keeps on. "Where is it? You're telling me we can't afford this, we can't afford that. Not even a lawyer? To make sure our daughter is protected?"

I knew we were hurting for it, but it sounds like it's gotten worse than that. How is that possible? Mom and

Dad have both taken more shifts in the last year than they ever did before.

"I just don't think," Dad says through gritted teeth, "that it's the best use of what we have."

"Right. Okay. God, I swear, if this is another—"

"It's not."

"Because I won't do it again. I won't stand by and—"

"Lower your voice, please. Our kid is down the hall."

"Yes," Mom says, "yes, she is." Like a challenge. Like a threat.

I hold my breath. Silence running like a tripwire through the house. I thought I knew the shape of this fight, but whatever they're talking about, it's more than money. Another, Mom said. Another what? What won't she do again?

And then I hear her sigh. "See, this is why I don't want to talk about it. There's nothing else to say."

Her footsteps, softly, down the hall. She's walking away, and for all that their fight was unfamiliar, now that it's over I can guarantee how things will go. Dad will walk down to the lodge to pick up Mom's car. Throw my bike in her back seat and drive out of town for a couple hours. When he comes back, he'll have a cold soda for me and one of those plastic-wrapped packs of cookies for Mom, bought at a gas station forty miles up the road. Mom will hide out in their bedroom. Go to sleep, and throw the cookies out when she wakes up.

That dinner I imagined, the three of us after the vigil if it had gone right. That's not how it would be at all, really. The fight still catches; the peace goes up in smoke.

I have never regretted what I did, and I still don't. But if Luce is alive, if the girls are all alive—if I didn't do what I'm sure I did—what would that even leave me with?

Slowly, I slip out of bed. Drop to my knees by the edge and peer into the darkness beneath it. Cobwebbed shadows knit tight, the carpet rough against my palms. Part of me is hoping it won't be there. But it is. A wooden box, the lid set with a bit of fake turquoise. I bought it years ago on a school field trip to the park in Bryce, the money lent to me from Edie. She never asked me to pay it back.

Since then it's where I stash the things I treasure most. A pressed orchid picked from the Eye. A keychain Dad gave me from the park—one of the nice ones, enamel, not plastic. And, since a year ago, two pairs of earrings. The hoops Jane was wearing that day, gold and simple and just big enough to fit on my little finger. Silver studs from Edie, a star and a moon.

They took them off before they went swimming: Jane because hers were real gold and she was worried she'd lose them, and Edie because Jane did. And when I tossed their clothes and shoes into the water, sent them down the siphon after their bodies, the earrings were what I kept. Safe in my pocket all the way home, because you can lie and you can scream, call me a leech and a spare part, but I'm still the one taking care of you.

I didn't keep anything of Luce's. Maybe if I had, I'd know what to make of her now.

I pick up the star stud, clutch it hard enough that the post nearly punctures my skin. I should get rid of these. Bring them out to the canyon tomorrow and toss them into the water when nobody's looking, or bury them in the desert behind those half-finished houses. Keeping them is just tempting fate.

And yet—

Luce is back. She slipped free of Devil's Eye. Came back from some hidden nowhere, took the hardest thing I ever did and made it disappear.

I drop the earrings back into the box and shut the lid. I need these souvenirs more than ever now. I need the hurt of them to know what's real.

I hardly sleep. Spend half the night fighting to breathe as the weight of the last two days bears down on me, canyon rock rising whenever I close my eyes. Finally, just before the first sign of morning, I give up.

Tiptoe, barefoot, into the hallway. From here I can see

Dad stretched out on the couch in the front room. I could go join him. Curl up on the floor, let the rising sun cast his shadow over me. He was the one next to me with the sheriff; he is the one meant to keep me safe.

I approach my parents' bedroom instead. Knock quietly on the door but don't wait for an answer before nudging it open and easing through. The darkness here is soft and woolen. Mom's shoes discarded by the side of her bed. A glass of water on the nightstand, a paper towel neatly folded next to it holding two pink painkiller tablets for her to take when she gets up.

"Mom?" I whisper, staring at her figure where she's curled under the rumpled duvet.

She doesn't move. Fear in my chest, flaring high and hot before guttering out. I can hear her breathing. I have not killed her too.

The carpet is rough under my feet as I inch toward the bed. How many times has Mom said she wants to rent a steam cleaner and get it looking nice again? How many times has she decided not to, in case that job pans out or that tourist boom happens and we can afford to move?

From the way she and Dad were arguing last night, I don't think we'll manage that anytime soon.

Standing at the edge of the bed, I can see her closed eyes, the length of her neck. The gray threaded through her blond hair. I look more like her than my father—that's what people say—but I cannot find myself in the kind line of her mouth.

She frowns as she pulls back the sheets. "Cold," she says. Voice muddy and sweet, still half asleep. "Come here."

Gratefully, I climb in alongside her. Let her draw the covers tight. Her arm hooks around my waist as I drop my forehead to her chest. Breathe when she breathes. She can teach me how.

Mom kisses the crown of my head. "Annie," she says, "my Annie," and then she's asleep again.

It cracks something open in me, makes me so desperately want to cry. All I can manage is a strangled little sound at the back of my throat.

Annie—that's the name she gave me when I was born, Ann Marie Carver, but I don't remember the last time anyone called me that. Always Nan instead, a rhyme from a nonsense song my father used to sing. For a long time it was his voice I heard when I introduced myself. Since last summer it's been Luce's. Nan, bright and bloody as it bounced off the cavern walls.

Does she remember that? I wonder as I shut my eyes. Does she ever hear it too?

THEN

Find midnight and keep on walking; follow a narrow road through the desert and it will lead you here, to a lonely hour at the edge of the lake. Water black and beckoning, the distant canyon silhouetted against the stars. The marina off to my left, and past it the beach and Bullfrog's, both still busy with a handful of tourists. I gave them a wide berth on my way down. Couldn't stand the scratch and howl of other voices after what happened at home.

It's supposed to be easier when Dad's back. That's what Mom always tells me during those weeks he's gone at work. Hang in there until he's home again; he can be the one to make dinner, to do the laundry. But since spring, if he's back in the house, it means an argument. Him and

Mom in their bedroom, fighting in whispers to keep me from hearing.

I dig my feet into the sand, down to where it's cool and dense. The best way to keep from hearing is to not be there at all.

I wish, sometimes, that I could talk about it with the girls. But Edie's parents are hardly ever apart. Jane's are so perfect that I'd be surprised if they've fought even once. And Luce's . . . we're not allowed to talk about her family. Not when everything with her mom is still so fresh.

I think she would understand, though, and that alone is a kind of relief. Too bad she's busy tonight. I looked through her window on my way down from the prefabs, just in case, but her bedroom was empty. Probably with Jane and Edie, enjoying what's left of the summer.

Soon you will be, too, I tell myself. Just get through a few more days. Then Dad heads back to Bryce, and you're free again.

From farther out across the water, the approaching rumble of a boat's engine. Too quiet to be a houseboat or a big cruiser. More likely a skiff, four or six seats, which means it's probably locals coming in to dock. I shrink back, grateful for the dark. I don't want any of my parents' friends telling them they saw me out so late.

But as the skiff draws nearer, the marina lights catch

the outline of the girl at the tiller. Her face obscured by the hood of her sweatshirt, but her tall, narrow frame all too familiar. It's Luce, and the two others in the boat with her must be Jane and Edie.

I get to my feet. Smooth down my hair, straighten my clothes, a smile already on my face. After seeing them in the Bristows' suite this morning, I didn't think we'd get to hang out again today.

Boards creak underfoot as I make my way down the dock, careful where the lake has covered the wood in a slick of algae. On one side, moorings for the lodge's houseboats—empty now, since the fleet is all being rented—and on the other, a row of slips. Luce has cut the engine now. Steers slow and easy toward the farthest slip.

"Hey," I call, waving. "Throw me the rope. I'll tie you off."

Luce waves back. A moment later one of the other girls stands up and tosses a coil of rope onto the dock. It lands with a thud. Starts to slide into the water, but I scramble for it, manage to grab it before it drops.

"Sorry," the girl says. Jane's voice, which means Edie's the one still lounging against the gunwale in the shadows. "My fault."

"I don't mind." Really, I don't, even though my knee stings where it dragged against the dock. This just isn't what Jane is good at. She's not like the rest of us, didn't grow up at the lake's edge.

The skiff drifts into the slip. I start winding the rope around one of the cleats. An uneasy prickle down my spine as I get a look at the logo printed on the stern. This skiff belongs to the lodge; Mom uses it sometimes when it's her turn to go check on the guests renting the houseboats. Luce must've taken the keys from their spot behind the front desk. If someone notices they're missing, lodge staff could get in trouble. My mom could—

I blink hard, stop the thought in its tracks. Everything is fine. We'll put the keys back before anyone notices.

I finish cleating. Stand up straight while Luce steps down from the boat, Jane close behind. Edie is last, but she hesitates at the gunwale. I offer her my hand.

"I've got you," I say. "Come on."

She takes it. My heart skips as her skin presses against mine. Lily-soft, water-smooth. I can hardly breathe, can only stare at her. What would it be like? Her body crowded close in the dark. The wet drag of her mouth down my neck until I pull her up, kiss her to dizziness, to dying.

If only, I think, our eyes locked. For a moment I swear she understands.

"Well?" Luce says. Edie and I both jump. "Are you getting off the boat or what?"

Edie climbs down onto the dock. When she lets go of me, it's slowly, as if she wishes she didn't have to. "Thanks, Nan," she says. "That was sweet."

Joy, fizzing and pink. My cheeks go hot, a helpless smile tugging at the corner of my mouth. I don't think she's ever been quite like this with me before.

"You're welcome," I say. Maybe she finally sees what I see.

"What are you doing out here?" she asks, brushing past me toward the other girls. Throws a look back over her shoulder. Sly, teasing. "Were you waiting for us?"

"I was just out for a walk." It sounds a little less pathetic than the truth, and besides, I know my parents would be pissed if I started telling everyone their business. "What about you guys? You went out to the canyon?"

Jane nods, and Edie says, "Yeah, to Devil's Eye."

Now that we're closer, I notice their damp hair, how Jane's shirt is clinging to her wet bathing suit beneath. A canyon swim—it's one of the best ways to spend a summer night. Luce is the strongest swimmer out of all of us, but Edie's a close second, and she loves it enough that she stayed on the high school team even after Luce quit. I bet she'd still be out there if it were up to her, floating on her back in the Eye.

"How was the water?" I ask her.

"Good," she says. "Really good. It's deep enough this year that you can dive off the side."

"That sounds awesome."

"It is," Luce says, pulling my attention back to her. "We need to make sure you can come next time."

Edie is quick to cover her surprise, but I catch it, hold it for a moment before it's gone. "Yeah," she says, nodding, "of course."

There it is, the summer I expected us to have, shimmering back into view. I grin. "My dad's home for another day or two, but maybe after?"

"Sure," Luce says, "we'll figure it out. But now we actually need to hurry. We have to get the keys back before shift change."

Edie rolls her eyes. "Killjoy."

"Yeah, that's me. Let's go."

They're both wrong, I think as I follow Edie down the dock. Luce isn't a killjoy. She's just worried, worried about everything, all the time. Getting in trouble at school or being late for her shifts at the gas station register. Worst of all, ending up stuck in Saltcedar, left behind by life just like her dad. And this year she's got something to lose. In two weeks' time, we'll be juniors, and she's been waiting for this year since we were small. Studying, practicing, pretending. I saw her report card at the end of last spring.

Class after class, a perfect grade, building herself a ladder to somewhere else.

That, I don't understand. I watch her lead the way down the dock with Edie and Jane, Saltcedar beyond, black velvet and gold. What else could I ever want?

We drop Jane off at the lodge, the keys in her care. Wait in the driveway outside until the light in her suite flicks on and off before starting up the road toward the prefabs. Toward home.

There's a chill in the air as we walk. End of summer bite and breeze. It makes Luce pull her hood up, tuck her hands into her sweatshirt sleeves. I keep so close to Edie that I can feel the heat of her body like a fire line down my ribs. Match my steps to hers, breathe only when she does.

I love the girls like nothing else, but Edie is different— her gravity stronger, the promise of her deeper, darker. It's been like that since the first time I saw her. Waiting for the school bus with Luce almost eight years ago now, the two of us watching as a new girl came traipsing up the road, not knowing how much things were about to change.

For the better, I think, as Edie's shoulder grazes mine. How lucky we were. How lucky I still am.

Take the right fork, where our street runs through the

prefabs. Edie's house comes up quick—hers is closer to the main road, with the other two-story models—but she doesn't peel off toward it. Instead she stays with us, and Luce doesn't comment, so neither do I. If Edie wants to spend more time with us, I'm all for it. Even silence like this is something precious.

It breaks only when we hit the last curve in the road. My house and Luce's both visible ahead, mine lit and hers left dark. Her driveway is empty too. Mr. Allard must be out. Bullfrog's, or another bar off the highway. Wherever he is, I doubt he'll be back before sunup.

"This is me," Luce says, as if we don't all know that already. "Good night."

"Good night," I answer, waving a little. We don't hug often; that's one of the few things I'd change, if I could.

Edie makes a low sound, her arms wrapped around herself. "Okay. See you tomorrow."

Luce sighs. "What?"

"Nothing. I'm just cold."

Should I invite her in? Offer her a jacket? But Luce is already taking off her hoodie and holding it out.

"Here," she says.

"Are you sure?"

"You'll need it to stay warm on that long walk home."

Edie rolls her eyes, but her touch is reverent as she takes the hoodie from Luce and puts it on. Her thumb running gently along the fraying at the cuff, her eyes soft and bright.

"Thanks," she says. "You're never getting it back, by the way."

"Yeah, yeah," Luce says, already breaking away. "See you."

Edie and I watch her head around the side of her house, wait together for the night to wrap her up. Luce always climbs through her bedroom window, sneaking in even though nobody's ever home to mind.

"What now?" Edie asks when Luce's footsteps have faded.

"I don't know," I say. Behind me, my own house, the memory of my parents' fight still lingering in the air. Why would I go back if I could be here with Edie instead? "I don't really feel like going home yet."

Edie smiles. I think I could turn the sky gold with it. "Me neither."

"Okay," I say. "So let's not go home."

At the very end of the street, past the last of the prefabs, a cul-de-sac lined with empty lots and one half-built house. This is what all the money was supposed to be for—a growing town, new jobs and better futures for all of us. But the lake started drying up and the money did, too, so the furthest they ever got with any of it was 11 Canyon Drive. Just a mailbox and the ground floor framed out. Kitchen island still wrapped in plastic. Plywood stairs leading nowhere.

We sit at the top of them, looking out at the neighborhood. Houses I've known all my life, near enough that if I yelled someone would hear, but it all seems miles away. The rest of my life on the lake's far shore while I sit here with Edie, wrapped in her shadow.

"Look," she says. "You can see Luce's house from here."

You can, and mine, too, but I don't want to talk about that. Not now that we're finally alone.

"It's a nice view," I say. "And the sky's really clear tonight. So many stars." Silence in answer, just the restless sway of Edie's shoulders as she fusses with the strings on her borrowed hoodie. I keep going to draw her out. "I wish I knew what all the constellations are called. We did that unit in middle school but I don't—"

"Do you have plans?"

I stare at her. Heart in my throat, hope waking fast. "For when? This weekend?"

"What? No. Plans for the future and shit." I flush, embarrassed, but luckily she continues. "We were talking about it in the canyon. Junior year and college and everything. Jane and Luce act like . . ." She draws her knees up to her chest. "Never mind."

"No." I shift closer. "Tell me."

"It's stupid."

"I'm sure it's not." She steals a look at me, unsure, like she's teetering just on the edge of the truth, about to fall. I push. "Seriously. I want to know."

For a moment I think she won't answer, but then she sighs, head bent low. "They act like it's real, I guess. Like all their plans are actually gonna happen. I guess they could. Jane has a million SAT tutors already and Luce is Luce. Even that shit with her mom didn't slow her down. And that's great. I mean, I'm so proud of her. But what about me? Will they just leave me behind?"

My heart clenches painfully. How could she think that? Doesn't she understand what she is to all of us?

"Edie, no," I say. "They would never."

"Yes, they would." A fever-gleam in her eyes as she faces me. "They will. I can't do the things they can, Nan. I'm not going the places they're going."

"You could," I offer, but she shakes her head.

"That's the thing. I don't even want to. I'm still here just trying to have a good fucking summer, you know?"

"Yeah. I really do."

Because I don't want to make plans either. I don't want to search the horizon for a way out of this town. No, I'd bury myself in Saltcedar if it meant I could be with my girls. With Edie, who's sitting here, silvered with moonlight and looking at me like I have a real chance.

You want a good summer, Edie? We can have that together. Right now, forever, a kiss in the dark, my heart in your hands and my name on your tongue. Will you let me, if I ask? Will you lean in to meet me? Closer, closer, and God, you're so beautiful I never even dream of you anymore—just of an emptiness where you're meant to be, like I know nothing of my own invention could ever match what's real.

"Edie," I whisper. I hear her calling to me; I only have to answer. "Edie, Edie."

My lips brush hers. Soft as sunrise but it's spark and fire and the start of the fucking world, like—

She pulls away. Eyes wide, her palm pressed hard against my shoulder for a moment until I lean farther back. "Nan," she says. "Stop."

Shame, crushing and cold. "Why? Was it bad or something?" I've never kissed anyone before. Maybe she could tell, and she wants someone more experienced.

"No, that's not . . . I mean, I—"

I laugh. "Thank goodness. I was worried I'd already ruined this."

"This?"

"Yeah. Us."

Edie stands up, stumbling a little on the plywood stairs. I reach out to steady her, but she's already too far to touch, her face cast in shadow by the streetlights beyond.

"Look," she says, "I think you might've misunderstood me."

"What do you mean?" But even as I speak, I can feel a slow wave starting to build. She doesn't want me to kiss her. She thinks I've misunderstood.

"Oh, fuck," I say. "You're straight?"

Edie practically chokes on her own spit. "Excuse me?"

"I'm so sorry." I get to my feet, my face burning with shame. "I didn't realize."

"Of course you didn't. I'm not."

It stops me short, hums like static behind my eyes. I don't understand. "So then what's the problem?"

"Nan," she says. Gentle, rueful, like she's looking down the barrel at a horse with a broken leg. "It's not that you're a girl, okay? It's that you're . . . you. And I like someone else."

Everything goes still. No heartbeat, no breath. Just Edie's words slipping between my ribs, and in the moment before I start to bleed, I can see it so plainly. The walk home. The borrowed hoodie. Edie on these stairs, watching Luce's house the way you watch the sky for shooting stars.

"Oh," I say. "You and Luce."

Edie winces. "I really thought you knew."

"Well, I do now." But that wave is cresting, breaking, and in its wake a riptide claws at my ankles, dragging me down, because even here when it's just me and Edie, there is always someone else. Always someone stepping in front of me and taking my place. Is that what I deserve?

Is this everything I'll ever have?

I shut my eyes so tightly I see bursts of purple, spirals and archways. My voice comes out scraped raw. "I think I'm gonna head home, actually."

"Nan—"

"It's fine. I'll see you later, yeah?"

I stare at the floor between us, at the nails in the plywood, the dust, the splinters—anything to keep from having to see her face. Please, just let me leave. Let me pretend that I'll be over this by morning.

"Sure," she says after a moment. "See you later."

I barely make it home before I start to cry.

NOW

The police boat is plenty big enough for my parents to have come along, but I'm glad I came alone. Mom couldn't miss work, no matter what she tried to tell me this morning. And Dad hasn't been back to the house since last night. Whatever mood he's in right now, I don't want to deal with it. But if I let Mom think he'd meet me down at the marina, well, what's a little white lie? I've told worse before.

And without their company, there's nobody to get between me and Luce. She's next to me on the bench at the stern, fiddling with the strap of her life jacket. Her eyes pensive, shoulders set like she's ready to take a hit. It's been this way since I showed up at the loading dock fifteen minutes early only to find her already there.

"A fun day out, huh?" I said. She didn't answer, but I let it go. We'd have plenty of time in the canyon.

Now I wish I'd pushed her. Asked her about her trip to the hospital, about the raw edges of her memory. I don't know if she'd have told me anything, but it would've felt good to get it out. As it is, I can feel it all gnawing a hole through me.

At least we're underway. The boat slicing through the chop, headed for the canyon arch. There's no backing out. This will be what it is until it's over, and then I won't have to think about it ever again.

"All right, girls. Anybody need any sunblock?" Sheriff Marsden is sitting on the bench opposite us, our reflections small and warped in her sunglasses. Behind us, another officer is at the wheel of the boat, the engine low as we scud across the deep.

"I'm wearing some already," Luce says. "You too, Nan?"

I nod, holding back a smile. Dead and gone for a year, but she hasn't changed. She burns as easily as I do.

"That's right," Marsden says, settling back, elbow propped up on the gunwale. "I forgot. You two are old pros at this. Nan, you come out here much lately?"

"Sure. It's hard to avoid the lake." She would know, wouldn't she? Marsden is still a Saltcedar girl, even if she hasn't been home since she was eighteen.

"The lake. Not the canyon, though?"

"I haven't been there since last summer."

"Why's that?" Marsden asks.

Because no day there will ever be as perfect as the day my best friends died.

"It's just been hard," I say instead. "But I feel a lot more up to it now that Luce is back."

"I'm glad to hear you say so."

"Why's that?" I parrot, catch Luce's amused smile out of the corner of my eye.

Marsden looks over her shoulder toward the canyon in the distance. The arch rising red and the slot beyond—a winding river, a garden on a string.

"It might be a tough day," she says as she turns around again. "For both of you girls. Nan, I'm sure this will bring up some bad memories. And we can only hope that's what'll happen for you, Luce." She swipes at the sweat dotting her forehead. "Plus it's already fucking hot out, if you'll pardon my language."

"We will," Luce says dryly. "Really, I think it'll be fine. I mean, you know I think this is a long shot, but I'm happy to help if I can."

Marsden grins. "That's the spirit."

I look away, leaving Luce to handle any further conversation. She's good with adults—teachers, coaches. They love how little she needs from them. How well she stands on her own.

I thought I might learn to be like that after the girls were dead, but I leaned on them anyway. I kept their memories close, kept those earrings in that little wooden box. Dreamed they were alive without ever dreaming I hadn't killed them.

Next to me, Luce shuts her eyes against the glare of the sun, and you really have to laugh, because it looks like I got exactly what I wished for.

We moor the boat at the arch, right before the lake funnels through it, turns to a little river running down the canyon slot. On a nice summer day, boats will drift here with their motors off. Old-timers napping in the arch's shade. Kids bobbing gently in their inner tubes, hooked together at the ankle so the current carries them together. So many marks carved in the rock—dates, names, initials. Some of them are even from back before the dam, buried by the flood for fifty years, now bared to the sun once more as the lake shrinks and the water drops.

I never left any marks of my own. None of us girls did. Why would we have needed to? Who could forget us?

But maybe Sheriff Marsden did. I scan the rock wall, searching for the right letters. How high would the water have been when she was young?

"Here we go," Marsden says. She stretches, wincing, as

she gets to her feet. "Luce, I don't suppose this has jogged anything in your memory? Any chance you can spare us the climb?"

Luce's answering smile is grim. "Sorry."

"Well, it was worth a shot."

Over the side, then. I gasp as the water hits my hips. The first inch of it is warm enough, but the cold is brutal below. Just like the Eye as I lured Edie and Jane in, the siphon waiting to call them its own.

I push on to shore, Luce at my heels, the two of us leaving the sheriff to ferry her climbing backpack across. The second officer, Marsden's deputy, will be staying with the boat, reachable by radio just in case. I pretended not to notice the look Marsden gave me back at the dock when she explained the plan for the day. A straggler left behind to wait—just like me in the story I fed her about how the girls went missing.

Maybe she's worried it's our turn to disappear.

Luce slips by me toward the trailhead, her eyes glassy in the morning sun. Is that fear I see, slowing her steps? Or joy, beautiful as barbed wire? A year ago I'd have been able to tell, but she's a stranger to me now. A ghost.

Look at me, I think. Prove you're real. You came back here and made a fucking mess of this; the least you can do is match your eyes to mine.

"Come here, girls," the sheriff calls. "We need to review the route."

Marsden has set her bag down and is crouched over a map of the canyon spread out on the dirt. I leave the trailhead, go to join her. The soft crunch of Luce's footsteps behind me as she does the same.

"Take a look," the sheriff says.

Luce and I kneel opposite each other, the map between us. I recognize it from the lodge; the Conservancy's got a rack of them set up at the front desk. More detailed than the kind you'd get from the Parks Service, but it's inane shit they've added. Where to spot an osprey, or where to find flowers you're actually allowed to pick. The only people who care about that kind of thing are the Conservancy volunteers.

Luce stares, rapt, at the map, and I'm reminded. Lucky us. We've got a volunteer of our own right here.

"Okay, Luce," Marsden says. "Can you show me the trails you guys would use?"

The old sheriff asked me the same thing last year. The canyon is too big to be searched in its entirety, so my bullshit answer determined where the divers and the drones spent the bulk of their time. No wonder they never found anything.

"Mostly the main slot," I interject before Luce can say

anything. "The basin, the southern ridge. All the regular tourist spots, right?"

She doesn't look up. But Marsden does, offering me a humorless smile.

"That's okay, Nan," she says. "I'd really like to hear from Luce." A gut-sick dread rolls through me as Luce stays quiet, still staring down at the map.

At last, she nods. Takes a breath, and as she does, my life ends—begins—a cataclysm in an instant, ripping everything to pieces. Is this it? Has it all come back to her?

"We used to go everywhere," she says. "But I think that day we were up in the cut."

I hold my breath, hope my panic doesn't show. That's a piece of truth I never, ever told, and judging by the look Marsden is sending my way, she wants to know why that is.

"The cut?" she repeats. "North? That's interesting. Can you show me where, exactly?"

Anywhere but there, anywhere but—

Luce reaches out. Taps the notch in the north slot where a trail splits off, snaking into the deep rock. "There," she says. "We used to go to Devil's Eye."

The name catches me like a punch to the gut. She remembers that much. Which means she might even remember that night. The horrible things the girls said to me. The choice I made. For a moment I swear I'm there, in the Eye up to my neck. When Luce tells Marsden the rest, it'll drag me all the way under.

But she doesn't. She only watches me, silent, impassive, until Marsden draws our attention with a heavy sigh.

"You have got to be kidding me," she says, shaking her head. "You girls really went up there?"

Oh, I think, of course. She'd know Devil's Eye, probably heard the same stories we did. She might have even found it herself.

"Sometimes, yeah," Luce says. "It's good swimming."

"It really isn't. There's a siphon at the bottom of that pool. You know that, right? It's incredibly dangerous. I mean, you shouldn't have been there at all, but to go alone, after dark?" The sheriff turns to me. "Is this why you said they went to the basin?"

I take the answer she's offering. Let it shape me into someone younger, with parents to be afraid of. "I thought they'd get in trouble if I told you. And then they'd be mad at me when they came back."

"Nan, do you realize—" Marsden cuts herself off. Pinches the bridge of her nose, her eyes squeezed shut. "Okay. We'll deal with that later."

She straightens to standing. I follow suit, leave Luce to fold the map back up. It's all right, I tell myself. Everything is all right. Marsden seems to have bought my excuse, and there are still plenty of ways this can break in my favor.

"Linney!" Marsden calls to her deputy on the moored boat. "We need to organize another search. Can you radio in and get things moving?"

I force myself to breathe steady. That's fine too. Bring in the search team. Bring the divers, the dogs, the drones. Hell, drain the water from Devil's Eye if you can. There's no evidence left there to be found. I kept everyone away long enough for the water to do its work.

"We're still going today, though, right?" Luce asks. "The three of us?"

Marsden nods. "If we can jog your memory and narrow the area down, that'll be a big help. But we'll have to go slow, all right? Stick exactly to the trails, leave everything as undisturbed as possible. Okay?"

"Of course." Luce smiles, relieved. "I'm just glad we're going."

So am I—I know there's nothing left at Devil's Eye, but I'm glad for a chance to double-check. Why does Luce care, though? What does she think is waiting for her out there in the canyon?

Maybe, I think, she's remembered the path she took that night, away from Devil's Eye to some beautiful, secret bower where she whiled away her missing year.

"Nan?" Marsden says. "Did you hear me? Take it easy and stay on the trail, yes?"

"Yeah, I got it."

I must not use the tone she was looking for, because she turns toward me, arms crossed. "I'm serious," she says. "The main slot gets a lot of foot traffic; if there *were* any signs of the girls down here, they're gone by now. But hardly anybody goes to the north slot, let alone all the way up to the cut. We might still be able to find something they left behind. If you set one foot off that trail, it better be for a good reason."

"Sure," I say, "but it's been a whole year. Even one day of rain could've—"

"We're not talking about footprints or a piece of litter." Marsden pauses, taking a breath. She is young enough still that I know where to look, how to spot the frustration seeping out the edges of her. "We'll start south of Devil's Eye. There's a spring there where the siphon lets out all kinds of shit."

"Excuse me?"

She grimaces. "Stuff. Sorry."

"No, I— What do you mean, lets out?" I say. "The Eye doesn't let out anywhere. It feeds right into the underground." That's why I did what I did with the bodies. That's why I let the siphon keep them—because I knew it would never give them back.

"It does and it doesn't," Marsden says. I try not to

shrink from the scrutiny in her stare. "When they dammed the river, the floodwater in that part of the canyon rose high enough to cover the outlet, so the siphon just carried right back into the subterranean system. That's how it was when I was your age."

"That's how it is now," I say.

"Could be, sure. But it's been a dry couple years and the lake's going down. Even in the span of a year I'd bet the water's dropped enough to dry that whole section out. So we can take a look, see what the Eye's been getting rid of."

Fuck.

Shiver and sway, the canyon around me tilting wildly as an image takes shape: Edie and Jane spat out the other end of the siphon, their corpses tangled up and left to rot in the sun. Waiting there, even now, for the sheriff to find, with my name carved into the backs of their skulls.

No, Marsden has to be wrong. Luce is the smartest person I know and she never said a thing about the siphon letting out. And even if it really does work like that, wouldn't someone have found Edie and Jane by now? A tourist lost on a hike, or a Conservancy volunteer making the rounds, or—

Or what? The searches stopped when winter set in. And the trails in the cut are usually flooded even into early summer, snowmelt pooling there from higher ground. These few weeks here, these hottest days—they're likely the only window anyone's had to properly check the cut. The girls have been waiting; it's finally time.

God, I was such a fool to trust this place.

But I did, and I'm here now, and I have to decide what the fuck I'm going to do. Marsden and Luce are going into the canyon. I could beg off, but they'll just send me home and go without me. Whatever time I buy myself won't be worth much in the end.

Every muscle in my body desperate to run, to drown, to die. All that will have to wait.

"Okay, then," I say. "Let's go."

We leave the boat behind, moored at the arch, Marsden's deputy lounging at the wheel with his radio on and ready in case we call for help. We won't need it, though. Whatever Luce does or doesn't remember, there's no way she's forgotten the canyon. Not after all that time at the Conservancy, all those tours and all that research. Summer after summer spent studying the canyon until she could map it with her eyes shut.

Does Marsden know it half as well? Did she have it memorized when the canyon belonged to her?

I don't think it ever really did. Watching Luce as we wade through the shallows, her sure steps, her easy balance, I can't imagine it being anyone else's.

Is that why it gave her back? Her, and not Edie or Jane, because she'd learned its every hidden pathway. Swum with its currents, climbed into its depths.

She's a few yards ahead of me now, poised on the crest of a submerged boulder. As I watch, she bends down, reaches into the river. Comes up with a rock in her hand. Beads of water winding down her wrist, the rock glinting white.

"Nan," she says, lifting her arm. "Think fast."

The rock arcs through the air, a comet cutting the sun in two. I catch it hard against my chest. Feel the edge of it dig into my palm. And one thought, too loud to ignore: it's about the size of the one I hit her with.

By the time I look up, Luce has already started walking again.

I drop the rock into the water. If I ever kill her again, it'll be with my bare hands.

NOW

North into the canyon, toward the cut. The walls rise steeply on either side of me—no shallows anymore, just cold, green water up to my waist. The river's surface is soft and furred with algae. It breaks around the sheriff's body as we walk, tadpoles below like black ribbons grazing my ankles; a dead fish, pink scales and wrinkled eyes, brushing my hip. A mosquito lands on my arm; I slap it. Someone else's blood leaks across my skin.

It smells rotten here. Stinging, sour. Too many people have passed this way, stirred the river and its banks—woken everything old and dying underneath. That's why we went up beyond the cut, to where sweeter air is waiting. The entrance to our route is coming up soon on the left, a little opening in the rock about a foot above the high water mark. Will Marsden know to lead us through? Did she learn, like we did, how to spot the oil-streak black of desert varnish across the stone?

"So, Luce?" she asks over her shoulder. "Does this look familiar? Are we on the right track?"

Luce drags her fingers along the water's surface. She's grown quieter the farther into the canyon we climb—quieter and lighter, almost, moving with a dream-drift reverence. It's enough to make me nervous. What are you thinking, Luce? What air are you breathing?

"Yeah," she says after a moment, "we definitely came this way. Didn't we, Nan?"

I stumble on a divot in the riverbed. Catch myself on the canyon wall, water sloshing up my ribs. The day before yesterday, in Jane's old room at the lodge, Luce said the last thing she remembered was the four of us in the skiff, heading across the lake. Has Marsden's idea worked? Is the canyon giving back the memories I took from her? Not the four of us in the skiff but here on this trail, climbing toward the end of it all. And whatever came after, in the span of those missing months.

"What do you mean?" I ask. Not a denial, but not a confession. I won't do this for her. Say it, Luce, if you're gonna say it.

"This is the way to Devil's Eye," she says. "So we had to have taken this trail that night, right?"

Marsden has fallen silent, but I can tell from the tilt of her head, from the angle of her body back toward us that she's paying close attention. Whether Luce meant to or not, she's laid a trap. Stretched the story I told Marsden across the trail to see if I'll trip over it.

"I guess," I say. "If you went to Devil's Eye, yeah."

She stops, twists around to meet my eyes. "If?"

"I don't know. I wasn't there, remember? I stayed behind on the boat."

The question hangs in the air. I offer her a smile, get nothing back. Only her stare, like a nail through my palm.

"Oh," she says at last. "I guess I just assumed you came with us."

"I wish I had. Maybe I could've changed it, and Edie and Jane would be here too."

A flash of something in her eyes before she keeps on up the trail. "Who says they aren't?"

As we enter the cut, we leave the river behind, and the canyon begins to change. Rose-colored rock and slices of shade carved from the sunlight. These trails used to be flooded by the lake—even five years ago we couldn't make it this far in without holding our breath and swimming through tunnels so tight they scraped at our ribs. Now the stone is worn water-smooth, and our steps kick up dust from the dried out riverbed, enough that I can feel it coating the roof of my mouth. We were soaked to the waist from the climb here, but our clothes dry quickly in the ruthless heat, only to dampen again with sweat as we maneuver up precarious scrambles, down threaded paths that narrow, slow our pace and funnel us together until Luce is right ahead of me. So close I could do it again if I wanted to. Just for old times' sake.

You might as well, I tell myself, the voice in my head taking on a slight hysteria. At the very least it's a surefire way to keep Marsden from reaching the siphon outlet. And hey, Luce might actually remember this one. Three for fucking three, right, Nan?

I shake my head, blink hard to keep the canyon solid around me. Blue sky streaked overhead, warping stripes of rust and orange pressing in as the rock rises high. There's still time. I can figure this out.

First, the rhythm of my breath—make it labored and shallow. Each step I take slower than the last, until I stop short. Brace with one hand against the canyon wall, the other clutching my side. Head bent low. No, lower, Nan. The picture has to look just right.

"Hey, guys?" I say. "Guys? I don't feel very good."

Luce stops hiking and turns around. I wait, but she doesn't double back to me. Doesn't say a word. I hope she can't tell I'm faking. Either way, though, it doesn't matter; this isn't for her.

"Luce? Nan?" Marsden's voice echoes down the trail. "What's going on?"

Luce raises her eyebrows, as if to say, "Well?" Beyond her, Marsden has begun making her way back toward us.

"Can we take a break?" I call to the sheriff. "I don't feel great."

"You don't?" Marsden sidles past Luce. As soon as she's near enough, she reaches out to steady me. "You do look a little pale."

"Don't worry about her," Luce says, all but rolling her eyes. "Nan just gets nervous when the trail is this narrow."

I clench my jaw. God, I would do anything to shut her up.

"Nervous, huh?" Marsden says to me. I don't bother arguing. "Okay. There's a clearing up ahead. We can take a beat and get you some air. Can you make it a little farther?"

"I don't think so," I say, just as Luce says, "Sure she can."

"I promise you can rest in just a few minutes." The

sheriff pushes her sunglasses up. It's embarrassing how reassured I am by the sight of her bare face, by her practiced calm. "Let's get there together, okay?"

She is not your ally, I remind myself. She's just afraid you'll get heat stroke and your parents will sue.

I lean into her anyway. Let her strength carry me up, my legs shaking with every step. Ahead of us, Luce is moving quickly, her body lean and strong, and we aren't there, not yet, but I wonder if she can hear it whispering to her—the place where she did and did not die.

Finally the trail opens, flattens. Before me spreads a clearing big enough for a campsite. A trickle-thin groove cuts down the middle, barely enough water draining through it to sustain the spray of browning tamarisk lining its edges.

"Here we are," Marsden says. "Come on, let's get you into the shade."

There isn't much this time of day—just a strip of it where the canyon wall casts a shadow. Marsden leads me over, settles me on a shelf of rock. Sweat in the crease behind my knees, muscles aching. It's been too long since I made this climb. I've forgotten what it takes from you.

Sheriff Marsden crouches to dig through her backpack. "I knew I should've brought more water." She tosses me her bottle, but I'm too slow, and it drops to the ground. It's Luce who picks it up. I wait for her to hand it to me;

instead she unscrews the cap and takes a sip. Pulls a face. Spits it out.

"Something wrong?" Marsden asks.

"The water's warm."

No shit, Luce. It's a thousand degrees out. But I say nothing, just grab the bottle from her and drink deep. Ignore the urge to make a face just the way she did.

"All right," Marsden says. She's started pacing, rubbing at the back of her neck. "Let's figure this out. It's about two hours from here back to the boat, conservatively. Nan, I don't want you moving more until you've had a good chance to rest, but I don't want us waiting too long. It's only getting hotter." Another glance at her watch, at the sun as it climbs toward noon. "Tell you what. You girls sit here for another twenty minutes and catch your breath. I'm gonna check just a little farther ahead."

Fear in a knot, tied tight behind my ribs. She can't keep going. Not without me there to steer her away from the worst. "That's okay. We'll come with you."

"Absolutely not."

"But—"

"You said you're feeling dizzy. That's probably dehydration." Luce makes a disparaging sound. Marsden ignores it. "I'm not letting you push yourself. You two stay here, and I'll leave you guys my radio. If I'm not back in twenty minutes exactly, you call the boat."

I want to keep arguing, but it might be better to stay on Marsden's good side while I can. And twenty minutes is hardly anything. How far from here can she even really get?

"I'm sorry," I say. "I know I'm being a pain in the ass."

"You want to find your friends. I get it. I want to find them too." Marsden pats me on the back; it almost doesn't feel patronizing. "But I think if they were here, they'd tell you it's important for you to take care of yourself. Right, Luce?"

Luce has gone to stand at the clearing's edge, her eyes closed as a slight breeze stirs her hair. "Right," she says, but she is not paying attention. I think she's listening to some secret song, to the canyon breathing in and out.

If I don't know how she's here right now, alive and well—if she really doesn't either—well, who's to say Edie and Jane left any bodies behind for Marsden to find?

"Okay," I say. "I'll stay here. But you promise just twenty minutes?"

Marsden nods. She takes off her radio. Presses it into my hands, along with a stopwatch she's fished out of her backpack. "I promise. I'll come right back."

I stare after her as she heads for the other side of the clearing, where the trail opens back up. Green light blinking on the radio, steady and soothing. The stopwatch's edge biting into my fingertips. I start it running before Marsden's even out of sight.

Hurry, I think, willing her to hear me. Hurry, so we can go the fuck home.

NOW

Dragonfly hum, the slip and rustle of the tamarisk. The air satin-soft as I catch my breath. This part of the trail is elevated enough that it never flooded more than a foot or two, and you can feel it in everything. A life, here. A vibrance. Plants growing thick down the walls, spared the strangle of the water. Small animals that will dart from their burrows when the sky gets dark.

It felt wrong, at first, to do it up here. Like I was breaking something sacred. But by the time Luce dropped to the ground outside Devil's Eye, I knew I'd misunderstood. This was sacred too. The blood on the rock, the hurt and the hunt. I looked at Luce's body and I called us what we were—kill creatures, born for exactly this.

She's watching me now from across the clearing, so I

take another long sip of water. Squint into the distance, hope she can't tell I'm counting the minutes until Marsden comes back.

"Okay," Luce says suddenly, "she's gone. You can drop it now."

"Drop what?"

"I'm so dizzy," she deadpans. "I think I'm about to fall down."

My cheeks go hot. "I was."

"Sure."

She wanders toward my end of the clearing, stopping in a sliver of shade. For a moment the canyon seems to bend toward her, and I'm convinced that if I split her open, I'd see red rock where her bones are meant to be. All those hours she's spent trying to find some way out of this town, find something better. She can keep trying, but I think she knows by now: she won't ever really get away.

"Did you already know about the outlet?" I ask. Is it a secret every good Saltcedar girl is supposed to keep?

Luce shakes her head. "I think the water's been high enough to block it since they dammed the river. People must've forgot it existed."

"Even the Conservancy?"

"I mean, there's probably something about it in their archives somewhere, but I never saw it."

That, I believe. Luce would never willingly pretend to know less than she really does.

"I wish I had, though," she continues. "If I'd known about it, I could've looked for that necklace I lost down the siphon two summers ago." She shrugs. "I guess it would've been too small to find. Not like a whole body or anything."

The breath rushes out of me. A flash in my mind's eye—Edie drowning in the Eye, Edie's hand reaching through my skin to hook around my rib and pull me down with her. "You think that's where the bodies are, then?"

Luce kicks idly at a stray rock. "It seems likely," she says. "You lost all three of us in the canyon, and it's where I showed up again. So I bet they're here too." Her brow furrows, the first sign she's at all bothered by this conversation. "Nothing ever really disappears, you know? I think it's always right where it was."

"What are you talking about?"

"It doesn't matter," she says, waving me off.

But it does, it does. Every word from her counts for the world, and these? Right where it was, she said. Right where—

"Luce," I say, "were you here?"

She raises her eyebrows. "Like, ever?"

Careful, Nan, a little voice warns me. Don't knock on a door you're not sure you want opened.

I don't listen. What's the point? I was careful when I killed Luce and look what good that did me.

"Like this past year," I say. "Were you here the whole time?"

Luce thinks for a moment. Cocks her head, but suddenly the angle's wrong, like her bones have snapped, and in a blink, blood is pouring from her skull. Slicking down her neck, streaked across her teeth.

"I told you," she says, voice hoarse like it's been ripped from the grave. "I don't remember."

I tear my eyes away, clench my jaw. Stare at the ground and will the moment to pass. I've been here before; I know this isn't real.

When I finally do look back up, the image has faded. The Luce watching me is alive again. Thoughtful, intent, a spark lit in her eyes.

"What?" I ask, dreading the answer. What pieces have clicked into place for her?

But there's no accusation. No memory dredged up from the depths.

"Your ponytail's coming undone," she says. Her mouth twitches, almost a smile. "I'll fix it for you."

I can't help shrinking back. "That's okay. I'll do it."

"Don't be silly. You're supposed to be resting."

"I mean, I think I can manage."

She ignores me, fishes a spare hair elastic out of her pocket before stepping up behind me onto the stone ledge. My skull cradled in her hands, skin prickling as she takes down my ponytail. I suppress a shudder of fear. If some part of her remembers what I did to her—if the pain of it lingers in her body, in her blood—here is her chance to give it back.

Sharp and delicate, her fingernail runs down the back of my scalp, parting my hair in two. One half she leaves hanging down my back; the other she starts to braid, working through the tangles more gently than I expected. Her knuckles brushing my temple as she adds a new lock to the braid with each twist of her wrist. I resist the urge to close my eyes.

"You know, I've always loved your hair," she says after a moment.

"Really?"

"Blond is so pretty."

"Thanks," I say. "Red is too."

Luce makes a small sound that might be laughter. "You think so?"

"Yeah. I actually had hair like yours when I was born, but it faded."

I don't know if that's really true, or if it's just something I might've heard my parents say once. I like the sound of it either way.

"Too bad," Luce says. "We could've matched. Here, hold this."

She hands me one of the hair elastics. With the other, she ties off the first braid. Flicks it over my shoulder so I can see. Smooth, tightly woven. Pleasantly heavy when I wrap it around my fist.

"It looks perfect," I say. "How'd you get it so neat?"

Luce runs her fingers through the other half of my hair. "Jane taught me," she says. "The first summer I met her."

"Really?"

"I knew how to do a regular braid already, but Jane did two Dutch ones like this on Edie, and Edie loved it so much she wore her hair like that all summer. Before Jane went back to Salt Lake, I asked her to show me how."

There's a soft melancholy in her voice, the closest thing to genuine grief I've heard from her since she came back. I wish I could tell her I never meant for this; she was never supposed to outlive them. That much, I really am sorry for.

"I bet Edie loved that," I say. I can remember it, too, if I try. Edie waltzing into school on a dozen different Mondays, two long, dark braids down her back.

"Yeah, she did." Luce has started on the other half of my hair, but a strand slips free; she starts over, more carefully this time. "It was nice. I really liked last summer, when we did that kind of thing."

"What kind?"

"All that cliché sleepover stuff. Doing each other's hair, painting our nails, talking shit." She pauses for a moment. Picks out a knot in the braid. "It felt like what best friends are supposed to do. Like we were all sisters, or something."

"We were," I insist. God, this is what nobody understands. "We still are. Just because they're gone doesn't mean none of that counts."

I love Edie and Jane, dead or alive. I love them smiling at midsummer or drowning in the dark. Everything Luce said to me that last day, everything she doesn't remember now—if I hadn't killed them, it all would've taken root.

This is how we keep our girls forever, Luce; this is how we love them right.

Silence, lingering just long enough that it begins to take a new shape. But then Luce taps my shoulder. "Elastic, please."

I give it to her, wait while she fusses. I think she must be almost done when suddenly her grip on my hair tightens—a quick, brutal yank, nearly ripping at the roots—and then it's over, like I might've dreamed it if not for the pain at the back of my neck.

"There," she says. "You're done."

No apology? No nothing? "Luce, what the hell? That hurt."

She steps down from the ledge. "The elastic got stuck."

Before I can respond, I hear footsteps up the trail. "Girls?" Marsden shouts, her voice carrying ahead of her. She's come back early.

Luce is watching me, something like a challenge gleaming in her eyes, but I look away. If Marsden picks up on any tension between me and Luce, it'll be one more hint pointing her my way—exactly the kind of thing I can't afford.

"It's fine," I say. It was just an accident. I have to get over it. "Never mind."

"Girls? Hello?"

Luce smiles and calls out, "We're here." Moments later, Marsden appears at the clearing's edge. Dripping sweat, breathing hard like she ran back here.

"You didn't have to rush," I say, standing up.

She doesn't respond, only strides across the clearing toward us, and I notice, suddenly, how unsettled she seems. Her face ashen, her hair coming free of its regulation knot. Shit. That's not the look of defeat I was hoping for.

"How'd it go?" Luce asks. Marsden doesn't even spare her a glance.

"Nan, where's the radio?"

I pick it up from the rock ledge, move to hand it to her before hesitating. Something happened. She found something, I know it. And I need her to tell me what right now, not in twenty-four hours after she's given a press conference. "What is it? What's wrong?"

"I need that, please."

"What happened?"

"Nan," she says, strained and rough. "The radio. Right now."

"But—"

"Oh, come on," Luce says. "Fucking give it to her."

I'm handing it over before I realize I've even moved. Instinct, I guess, to do as Luce says. I wish that were a habit I could break.

Chirp and static as the sheriff radios her deputy. "Linney. Linney, come in. It's Marsden."

His answer is quick. "Yeah, I hear you."

"I need everybody to the canyon, as fast as possible." Marsden hesitates, her eyes meeting mine. I swear I can see the moment she decides to say it, to let me hear what she's found. "Forensics, search, the whole deal. I've got remains up here. Skeletal. At least one set, but it looks like there could be more."

I'm conscious of my knees buckling, of Marsden catching me around the waist and sitting me down. And I can feel my mouth moving—I'm talking to her, I'm telling her I feel fine—but for a moment, all I can see is a dark stretch of road, Edie and Jane ahead of me as we walk toward the lake. Jane's humming her favorite song. Edie's got a bruise on the back of her calf and I know the shape of it like I know my own name.

"I'm sorry," Marsden says. Her hand is strangely cold against my cheek. "I wanted a better end for this."

We might still have it. The remains might not be theirs. They could be lost hikers from decades back. Bodies carried downriver from hundreds of miles away.

But I don't really believe that, do I? Send up a signal flare. Tie a yellow ribbon across the trail—caution, do not cross, because there, on the other side, the canyon is letting go of what it no longer needs. A pink bikini strap. A string of vertebrae and a jawbone studded with teeth. Edie and Jane, home at last.

THEN

Morning falls like an axe. Time to get up, Nan. Open your eyes, watch yourself bleed out.

The worst part is that I know she meant it. You're you, she said. You're you and that's the problem. You're you and not Luce.

I roll out of bed and stagger into the kitchen, Edie's voice chasing after me. It's later than I thought, nearly noon, and the house is empty, the only sign of anybody an empty coffee mug in the sink. Mom will be at work, but I'm not sure about Dad. He's hard to pin down when he's not in Bryce.

I peer out the front window. His truck's not in the driveway; across the street, Mr. Allard's is gone too. Are they off somewhere together? Boat engine idling, the two of them splitting a six-pack while they wait for the fish to bite?

No—those days ended this past spring. Mrs. Allard left a note behind when she skipped town, a goodbye typed up nice and neat, but the police still showed up at the Allard house. Still dragged Luce's father out by his elbow and took him to the station in Bryce so he could tell them where he'd hidden his wife's body.

I can still hear how he screamed that night. I never hurt her, he cried. She's out there somewhere. Find her, please. I miss my wife.

Even now, after four months without a body, nobody believes him. Except Luce, who watched from her front steps as the police took him. I was standing at the edge of the street; I remember I waved. And I think she saw me, but she didn't wave back.

She should have. That's how it ought to work—her body not her own but a reflection in my mirror, moving when I move. Smiling when I smile, because we're the same, aren't we? Our dads worked the same job until Mr. Allard got fired. Our houses built from the same blueprints, our clothes bought from the same consignment store. The same fucking classes at the same fucking school, everything, all of it, except for some reason, Luce is the one Edie wants.

For some reason, I'm not her.

A ripple through my muscles, venom setting in sweet. Don't worry, Edie. I can fix that.

Gas station door swinging open, air-conditioning raising goose bumps on my legs as I step inside. I had to wait hours for this. Until the sun sank low, until the sky went pink, because Luce usually works afternoons at the cash register and I can't get what I came here for if she's watching.

Luckily, I timed it right, and it's Glen behind the counter instead. He doesn't even look up from his phone when the bell hanging from the door jingles, or when I pass in front of the register before ducking down the aisle. Products are sparse on the shelves, but that's nothing new. This is just where any overstock from the convenience store by the lake ends up, discounted for the odd passed expiration date or broken safety seal.

I head for the far end of the aisle, my pulse beating louder and louder. I swear I saw them here once: boxes of hair dye stacked between the bargain bin makeup and the shampoo, the model on the front of each one promising fresh color in only five minutes. If they're all gone, I don't know what I'll do. If I can't—

But there they are. Relieved, I drop to my knees in

front of the shelves. Push aside the wrong shades, the blond and the black and the dark brown, until I can get my hands on it. That one box of red, labeled Ruby Blaze in peppy, bold font.

I carry it up to the counter with trembling hands. Here is something precious. Another step closer to the picture of Luce that hangs in my mind's eye. Another step past what Edie said last night.

"That's it?" Glen asks when I set the box down in front of him. "Anything else?"

"No, I'm set."

He rings it up. I pay in cash. The change is cold; it sticks to my palm.

"Hey, hang on a second," he says. "You live over by the Allards, right?"

"Yeah, why?"

He pulls an object out from under the counter. Luce's phone. I recognize its lilac case. "Can you get this to Luce? She left it here during her shift."

"Sure," I say. I'm trying not to stare at it but I can still feel myself leaning in. "I'll probably see her later."

"Okay, great. Thanks."

He passes the phone over. An eager shiver runs through me at the feel of it in my hand. Here are Luce's words, her friendships, her secrets. Her whole life in one thing, and Glen's just given it to me like I'm doing him a favor.

"No problem," I say. Snatch the box of dye off the counter and head for the door, my heart pounding, mouth split by a wild smile.

I came here looking for a way to get closer to Luce. To step into her body as best I can until Edie has no reason to want anyone but me. And now I have everything I need.

I set it up like a ceremony. The box opened, the contents laid out neatly on the edge of the sink—a pair of plastic gloves, a brush, a tube of dye. A beach towel nobody will miss draped around my shoulders and my favorite outfit hanging on the back of the door for me to put on after I'm done.

And still in my pocket, Luce's phone. I can feel the edges of it digging into my thigh.

I meet my reflection's eyes in the bathroom mirror and smile. Later. First things first.

I tie my hair back, leaving out a test strand at the nape of my neck. Luce's color is tricky—feather and fire, light without being pale, almost translucent in the sun. I'll need to be careful to get it just right.

My hands tremble as I slip the gloves on. Skip the brush, squeeze some dye out onto my fingertips. It's cold even through the plastic, and it squelches as I card it through my hair. Red over the blond, more saturated with every pass, foaming near the ends.

The color is darker than I thought it'd be. Heavy and faded like old blood.

It's okay, I remind myself. Don't worry. It'll show up different once it's rinsed out and dry. I just have to wait a little until it's ready.

Turn away from the mirror, the weight of my reflection's stare following me even as I sit down on the edge of the bathtub. Pull off the gloves, let them drop into the tub. The dye will stain but I can't bring myself to care when it's finally time to look at Luce's phone.

I pull it out of my pocket. The screen is warm, fingerprints smudged across it. Most of them will be Luce's, but by now some of them must be mine, too, and the thought is enough to leave me dizzy. This belongs to me; she belongs to me.

Who does she talk to that I don't know about? Does she write notes for herself, make lists? What kind of pictures does she take? I will never have to wonder again.

I've watched her unlock her phone a million times, so it only takes two guesses before I get it right. The passcode is a vaguely familiar number. Her mom's birthday, maybe. That wouldn't surprise me. And neither does the look of her home screen. Folders labeled and sorted, her calendar and to-do list both intensely color-coded. Not a single unread message—even her news alerts are cleared—and the background she's chosen is white.

Just white. No picture, no words. "What?" I can imagine her saying. "I don't like distractions."

I roll my eyes, open her texts and find Edie's name, the conversation second from the top. I need to see what she and Edie talk about. Learn it like a script to follow.

But my thumb hesitates over the screen, eyes drawn in by Luce's most recent message: "I'm serious Luce. You need to stay away."

Who the hell is texting her like that? Luce hasn't saved the number under any name, and I don't recognize it other than the area code. Someone from school?

I can't help it. I open the thread. It's short, the whole conversation visible on the screen at once, and the earliest message is from only a few days ago.

We need to talk.

how did you get my number

Pick up.

After that, the next morning:

I thought we had an agreement.

Luce doesn't answer. The next message from the stranger is stamped with today's date.

There's no reason to involve her.

I'm serious Luce. You need to stay away.

or what

I stare at Luce's reply, stuck somewhere between worry and laughter. Of course Luce isn't afraid—I'd expect nothing less—but that doesn't mean this isn't something frightening. A stranger, threatening her, and over what? Who is she supposed to stay away from?

I run the summer back in my head. Comb through the last few days moment by moment, but there's nothing out of place, nobody she's been talking to more than normal. I could ask her about it, but I don't think that would get me anywhere. After all, if she hasn't told the rest of us about this yet, why would she decide to share now?

Unless she's told the others, and I'm just the last one left in the dark.

I close the thread. Scroll back through Luce's inbox, looking for her thread with Jane. As I search, the phone buzzes in my hand and a notification appears on the screen. It's a text from Edie. My breath catches; I tap through to read it without a second thought.

It's a picture. Edie on her back in bed, wearing Luce's borrowed hoodie as she flips the camera off. After only a moment, another text comes through, this one just the message: "keeping it sorry"

God, she looks beautiful. Dark hair long and tangled, eyes heavy-lidded. What I wouldn't give to be the one she wants.

You will be, a small voice tells me. You almost are.

I stand up. There she is, my own reflection waiting in the mirror over the sink. As I watch, she looks down at the test strand of hair hanging over my shoulder, the dye coating it now dried to a crust.

She's right. The threats on Luce's phone, the picture of Edie—none of it's worth upsetting myself over. I'm getting closer to Luce with every second, and when I'm finished, her life will be mine to live. I won't have to ask about that stranger's texts, because I'll know it all, every secret of Luce's sorted and folded in a box under my bed.

I run the tap as cold as I can stand. Bend low and work the test strand under the water until the dye begins to run. Faster, faster, it pours down the drain. Did I use too much? Will there be any left behind, or did I mess this up?

I bite hard on the inside of my cheek. This will work. It has to. If it doesn't—

If I'm still myself—

If I'm still Nan, I think I'll scream.

The water runs clear at last. I shut off the tap and wring out the test strip, trying not to look too closely as I do. Yes, it's paler than I wanted, but I can just add more dye when I do my whole head. And when it dries, it'll look different. No, perfect. It'll look perfect.

Only it doesn't. It's just my same hair, patches stained with a horrible rusty pink. It's just the same girl as always.

If I'm still Nan, I think I'll scream, and here I fucking am.

A text to Luce from Edie's number, just past sunset:

this is luce allard can whoever has my phone bring it to my house already thanks

Screen door slamming shut behind me. Luce's phone in my pocket and her house lit up opposite mine. Everything's going to be fine, actually.

I know what I'll tell her. Sorry, with a little smile. I meant to get it back to her sooner, but I had to help my mom with her afternoon shift. Turned down a few beds, washed a few dishes. Yes, I remember every moment of it exactly. Why wouldn't I when it's what happened?

Still, I check that my hair's tied up tight on my way across the street. No reason. It just never hurts to be sure.

Mr. Allard's truck is in the driveway, so I veer left around the side of the house the way I've seen Luce do when he's home. If she's not in her room, I can just jimmy the window and get in myself; our houses are the same prefab model, so her window's got the same hitch in the framing as mine.

But she must be home. A lamp's on inside, gold spilling through the glass, beckoning me closer. I obey. Press ahead toward the light. The window ledge hits almost shoulder-high for me, so I can see a sliver of her room. The calendar she's got hung over her bed, her shadow on the far wall. The corner of her dresser just in view. Her things, her space, her life, all just like mine, only she's the one who—

Something writhes in my chest, shrieking, wailing. I can't imagine what it could be. No, I have everything I've ever asked for. I am so happy I could cry.

I run my hand over my hair, tuck the ends more deeply into the knot. Put on a smile and step into the fall of light.

Luce isn't alone. Edie and Jane are with her, Edie sprawled on Luce's neatly made bed while Jane riffles through Luce's closet. Luce herself is sitting at her desk with her back to the window, her open laptop at her elbow.

My dad's not home, so they know I'm free. But I bet they told Edie to text me and she forgot to, as usual. Everyone knows if something needs doing, you give it to Luce, and she couldn't very well text me when I've got her phone.

"Jane, stop," she's saying now, her voice carrying through the gap where the window's cracked open. "You're being so distracting."

I should knock, let them know I'm here, but there's something about this—watching my girls like figures in a snow globe, like looking into a chamber of my own heart. I can't tear myself away.

"I'm just trying to help," Jane says. "You said you needed an outfit for the party." She frowns, pulls a dress out of the closet. "Get rid of this, Luce. It's so boring."

Plain black, long sleeves. I recognize it. Luce wears it to her honor society awards ceremony every year.

"Put it back," Luce says.

"No, come on. When would you ever wear this?"

"Jane, for real. Put it back." Luce was laughing before; she isn't now. "I need it."

"What for? You have a lot of funerals coming up?"

"Maybe. You heard from my mom lately?"

Jane's face falls. Cheeks red, eyes wide. I can see the breath she takes, hear it hitch. "I . . . I'm so sorry. I wasn't thinking."

Silence, gripping us all tight. Come on, Luce. She didn't mean it like that.

Finally Luce's posture seems to relax. "How about I just borrow one of your dresses?" she says. Apology accepted; Jane smiles, grateful but still mortified. "It'll be too short on me, but I don't mind."

"Oh, you'll be fine," Edie teases. "Jane's shortest dress still covers her knees."

"Hey," Jane protests, "they're—"

"Church dresses. We know."

"That's all my parents will buy me."

"Wow, I'm sorry." Luce nods to the black dress where Jane left it hanging. "Want to wear that instead?"

Jane is blushing so hard I think she might burst into flames. "Shut up," she says good-naturedly. "I hate you both."

Luce laughs, flips Jane off, and turns back to the desk just as I lift my hand to knock on the window. For a moment our eyes lock, computer glow painted white across her skin.

"Fucking hell." She recoils. "Nan?"

"Sorry!" I wave to Edie and Jane over her shoulder. "Sorry, sorry. Did I scare you?"

"Just a little." Luce gets up and kneels on her desk chair. Opens the window the rest of the way. "What are you doing out here?"

"Bringing your phone over."

"Oh, thanks."

She reaches down to me; I grab her hand, use it to help boost myself up onto the window ledge. Swing my legs over the same way I climb into my own room, only Luce's desk makes it tricky. I almost send her laptop tumbling onto the floor, but she steadies it in time.

"I have a front door, you know," Luce says.

"I wasn't sure if you were home. Hi, Edie."

Edie's staring at me from the bed. At the sound of her name she blinks, pushes herself upright.

"Um, yeah," she says. "Hi."

I can't place it, at first. The tension in her body. Her unusual stillness, like she doesn't want to be noticed. But then it hits me. She's nervous. She must think I'm holding a grudge over what happened last night at the abandoned house. Our almost kiss, and what she said to me afterward.

Oh, Edie. I'm not angry; I couldn't be. All you did was tell me what you want. And I'm working on it, I promise.

But I can't say that out loud, not with the others here, so I cross the room, sit down next to her on the bed. This way she'll know everything's cool with us.

"What were you guys doing?" I ask, all too aware of Edie's body next to mine. "Picking outfits for tomorrow night?"

Jane nods. "What are you gonna wear, Nan?"

"Probably just the same dress as last year." The

end-of-summer party is an annual thing, and while it's fancier than most Saltcedar events, it's certainly not fancy enough to warrant buying new clothes. "Can someone do my eyeliner before, though? I always fuck it up."

Luce looks up from her desk, where she's been sorting the papers I disturbed on my way in. "Yeah, I can do it before we walk over."

Edie makes a strangled sound under her breath. God, relax, I think. Luce and I aren't like that with each other even in the slightest.

"Actually, Nan," Luce goes on, "random question, but do you know anyone on the East Coast?"

"What?"

"Extended family? Your parents' friends?"

What does that have to do with anything? I glance at Jane, but she seems equally confused.

"I don't think so," I say. "Why?"

"No reason." Luce doesn't look away, though; if anything, she watches me more closely as she adds, "It's just something my mom said in her letter."

The one she left on Luce's nightstand, slotted neatly into a plain, white envelope. I know a little about the contents—the goodbye, the apology—but Luce has always been careful to keep the specifics to herself. Even now, I'm not quite sure what she means.

"Something about me?" I ask.

Luce shakes her head. "The coast. She said that's where she's going. I thought if you knew anyone, maybe . . ."

Maybe they've seen her. Maybe they can send her home.

"Sorry," I say. "I can check with my parents, though."

"Yeah, sure." Luce stands up abruptly. "Okay, I'll see you guys tomorrow."

Jane and I both start moving, used to Luce's particular kind of dismissal. Honestly, with the way she likes ditching early, we're lucky she didn't sneak out and leave us alone in her house.

Edie, though, isn't budging. She sinks deeper into Luce's bed. Pulls a pillow over her face, and from beneath it, stifled but still plaintive: "Come on. It's barely nine."

"Too bad," Luce says without a smile. "I'm tired."

I step over a stack of schoolbooks and follow Jane to the door. Edie will draw this back-and-forth out as long as she can, and I guess that's fine. After all, I can't offer her what she's after just yet. But I will soon, and until then, I don't have to watch whatever bullshit she chooses to keep busy with.

"Hey."

"Yeah?" I whirl around. Has she changed her mind?

It's Luce, her palm outstretched. "You forgot to give me my phone."

"Shit, yeah. Here."

I fish one out of my pocket. For a moment I'm not sure if it's hers or mine—lilac case held tight in the bathroom light, texts from that stranger all across the screen—and then Luce grabs it, flicks quick through her notifications, and I could ask her right here, right to her face.

"Thanks," she says. Turns the screen off, tosses her phone onto her bed. "Okay, see you tomorrow."

"Sounds good," I say, and I walk home smiling. What was there to ask? Nothing's happened; everything is just fine.

NOW

A breeze slices across the lakeshore. Quiet punctured by the call of a bird perched somewhere in the scrub. I shiver, tuck my hands into the sleeves of my sweatshirt. It would be warmer down with everybody else, crowded into the lodge parking lot for another press conference, but I'm watching from the little rise across the street, balanced astride my bike, ready to break for home at a moment's notice. I'm not even supposed to be out of the house, never mind this close to the circus. But I couldn't let it happen without me.

This morning's headline takes shape in my mind. REMAINS IDENTIFIED—JANE BRISTOW, 16, EDIE GALE, 16, CONFIRMED DEAD. It took a week for them to be sure. A team at the outlet day and night, gathering up the girls bone by bone. Then tests at a lab in Salt Lake, because of course the Bristows know the medical examiner there. And all the while, I lay empty-eyed in bed, listening to Mom shoo reporters off our front steps.

Until last night. Until the voicemail the sheriff left on my mother's phone, sharing with us what I already knew. Yes, it's them. No, we're not sure how they died.

That's what the Bristows and the Gales are telling the press right now. The police arrayed behind them as they lean in, make sure the microphones pick up their tears.

I thought I might cry too. After all, there it is, going up in smoke—the world where Edie and Jane survived just like Luce did, where it's all undone and I'm not the girl who killed her friends. But then, I never wished myself away from that girl. I held her close; I dreamed of her. And since Luce came back, I've had to wonder if that girl was ever real.

Now I know for certain. Mom played that voicemail for me and I told myself, Thank God. Edie and Jane died just the way I meant them to. At least part of that day was true.

That bird calls again. I recognize the sound; it's a mourning dove. They're all over Saltcedar, no matter the season. Early, before I have to get up for school, mist and sunrise and a sweet, sorry song. At this hour, most of them are off settling down to sleep, but this one is here and it's singing to me like I'm something to mourn.

I search for the shape of it in the scrub. It's not an omen or a judgment—I know that. It's just a bird awake a little later than it's meant to be. But I have to see it to be sure. Everything is something else lately.

It takes me another minute, another song, until I can spot the dove. A rustle of wings in the scrub oak, beady eyes glinting as it watches me. Its body is small enough that I could capture it in my fist. Like Luce that day, out in the desert at the end of our street. The half-dead bird, a coyote's yellow eyes watching from the dark as she snapped its neck.

Could I do the same? Picture it. My grip too tight—the dove like a paper crane, skeleton crumpling, the membranes of those eyes popping—not to spare it pain but to see what it would feel like—

My stomach clenches. I look away, back toward the lodge across the street. Disappointment bitter on my tongue. I should have enjoyed that. It's what we do, isn't it? People like me? We leave warning signs behind, proof for people to point to when they say we've always been this way. No reason, no regret.

Only I did have a reason, didn't I?

It's just that sometimes—for an instant, for a second,

right on the edge of nothing as I'm falling asleep—I can't quite remember what it was.

One last look at the scene in front of the lodge before I ride home. Those people with their microphones and their cameras, the crowd like thunder, camera-flash lightning—last year it made me laugh. All anyone wanted was to know what happened, and I already did. But we have some of the same questions this summer, don't we? Everyone's trying to understand how Luce survived what the other two couldn't.

I kick off, start pedaling back up the road. By all means, I think, ask away. If Luce is holding on to any answers, she's not sharing them with me.

I reach the top of the hill. From here I can coast all the way to the prefabs. Right up to my doorstep, where my mom will likely be waiting. She'll yell at me for sneaking out, and she'll lecture me about photographs and gossip. Strain leaving new creases by her eyes, tugging at the corners of her mouth.

That, I am sorry for. Especially now that Dad's back at work in Bryce, and she has to handle all of this alone.

Lean forward, let my momentum carry me past the welcome sign, past the turnoff for the fire station. There's the gas station ahead and the billboard looming over it.

My girls framed by the sunset sky, Edie's smile so bright that even now I can't help but give one back. And standing at the base, in the billboard's shadow, a girl astride a bike, one foot on the ground keeping her balanced. Blue dress, red hair hanging down her back. Luce.

I brake hard. Skid to a halt across the street from her, and I'm sure she hears me, but she stays where she is, her gaze fixed on the billboard. On her own face, caught in the middle of a summer smile.

I could call out to her. Tell her I did the same thing the day she came back. Stood right where she is now. Missed her, and meant it.

There isn't time. An engine gunning from down by the lodge, the silence cracking. Luce whips around, and our eyes meet—the moment drifts—between here and there, between living and dead—

Blood running riot through the canyon cut. Where were you, Luce? Where, where, where—

I gasp. Catch my breath as the engine growls again and a car passes between us. No, not a car. A county police cruiser, its lights and sirens off. They must be heading back to Bryce now that the conference is done.

Except they go right at the fork. Toward the prefabs. Toward my house, and Luce's too. And as they round the corner, I spot who's at the wheel: Sheriff Marsden.

My mouth goes dry, a prickle running down the back

of my neck. Something's going on. I need to get home fast, and so does Luce.

We ride together. Not a word between us as we trail the cruiser, but I can feel Luce looking at me. Does she know what this is? Has she remembered everything and called Sheriff Marsden to my door?

No, no, she hasn't, because the cruiser turns left, into Luce's driveway instead of mine. Mr. Allard is already standing on the front steps, his face grim and too pale. When Luce pulls in just behind the cruiser, he reaches out to her. Says, "Lucy, come here," and I think he might be about to cry.

Luce darts up the steps to join him. I park by my mailbox and watch Marsden get out of the cruiser. An uneasy hum in my ears, stronger and stronger as she takes off her hat and climbs the front steps to where Luce and Mr. Allard are waiting. This can only be bad news.

They are too far away for me to hear all of it, but I hear enough. That the bones they found in the canyon were Edie's, yes, and that they were Jane's, but that there were others. Bones that didn't belong to either girl, and Sheriff Marsden is so sorry—she is just so sorry, she cannot imagine—but she has to tell them: they belong to Maggie Allard. They belong to Luce's mother.

NOW

Black dress on my bedspread, the tags still on. I stare at it from the doorway, clutch the towel wrapped around my body. Mom must've bought it for me. Laid it out while I was in the shower.

I leave wet footprints on the carpet as I approach. Run my fingers along the dress's hem. It's real fabric, with an actual weight to it. Nicer than anything I have in my closet. The size is wrong, though. It would've fit me last summer, but I've grown.

Mom got it back then, didn't she? She knew. Edie and Jane were dead, and one day their bodies would come home to be buried, no matter how many candles we lit for them or how many hours we prayed.

The dress slides over my skin, the zipper cold down my spine. It'll close if I hold my breath.

"Nan?" comes her voice from the kitchen. "Are you making progress?"

"Yeah."

"Because we have to leave early, remember?"

"I said yes."

The church the Bristows and the Gales picked is closer to Bryce than Saltcedar, so Mom and I are picking up Dad from work on the way to the funeral. He's hardly been home since they found Jane and Edie—just a pit stop to pick up clean clothes and give me a kiss on the cheek before he went back to work. I don't think he even said hi to Mom.

It all surprised me at first: the joint ceremony for the girls and how quickly it came together, along with the fact that the Bristows wanted to bury Jane down here, and not up near them in Salt Lake. But Mom reminded me—these two families have had a year to plan. And Saltcedar was Jane's favorite place. They'd probably have buried her in town if we had any kind of cemetery.

Selfishly, I'm glad we don't. I'll remember Jane and Edie well enough without having to bike past their headstones.

Outside, a car starts, rumbles out of the prefabs. Another family leaving for the funeral. The whole town will probably be there—the only people I'm not sure about are the Allards.

I haven't laid eyes on either Luce or her father in two days, not since Sheriff Marsden broke the news about Maggie. Instead, I've watched from my own front window as their house swarms with police, all hunting pointlessly for clues that might explain how Maggie's body ended up out in the Eye, her bones mixed in with Edie's and Jane's.

"Hey."

I jump. Mom's in the doorway. Her lipstick already coming off, wrinkles setting in her black skirt.

"Hey," I say. Smooth my hands down over my own dress. "Do I look okay?"

She nods. Eyes tired and soft as she smiles. "You look lovely, sweetheart."

"Okay. I'm ready, then."

"You have everything? You have what you're reading?"

"In my bag." The Bristows asked me to be part of the ceremony yesterday. Told me they wanted me to read Jane's favorite poem verse—I had to hide my surprise, because I didn't think she had one—and that the Gales were asking Luce to do the same for Edie. I can't imagine she said yes, though. Luce just lost her mother all over again. Nobody would blame her for sitting this one out.

I almost wish I had her excuse. Each minute that passes drags the ceremony closer. I'd snatch them all back if I could, stay here in my room where the light is thin and cold.

"Are you sure we can't just meet Dad at the church?" I ask. It wouldn't buy me much time, but I'll take what I can get.

"Yes, Nan," Mom says. A muscle jumps at her jaw. Cheeks flushed. "I'm very sure."

"But wouldn't it be easier for him to just take his truck? Bryce is at least twenty extra minutes, and—"

"Nan? We're picking him up." The sharpness of her voice seems to startle us both. For a moment she only stares at me, and then she's sweeping me up in a hug. "I'm sorry," she says. "Today's a hard day."

I shut my eyes, press my forehead to the crest of her shoulder. "Yeah, I know."

"I wish there were something I could do to prepare you, or make it easier."

I can feel it in the tightness of her hold on me, in every twitch in her body. She's frightened. Sad and angry, too, but more than anything else, she's scared down to the marrow.

"Mom?" I hesitate. There are some questions too dangerous to ask. This one comes out anyway: "Is something going on?"

"No." She smiles, but it fades quickly, leaving behind care so sincere that I almost can't bear to look at it. "I just . . . you know I'd do anything for you, right? Anything. I mean it."

And I do know that. My mother loves me; I can always tell. Usually, though, it comes out differently. Food waiting for me in the fridge, or two weeks straight with no day off work just so she can take one on my birthday. Not this, her face so close to mine, words pulled from a part of her she usually keeps secret. What did I do to earn it?

Luce's voice, whispering: Take a fucking guess.

It runs through my mind frame by frame—Mom finding my bloody clothes in the laundry, Mom crying alone in the staff room before drying her eyes and going back to her desk. She'd stand between me and the world if I asked her to. She'd do the same if I didn't.

But none of that ever happened. The clothes I wore that day are gone; I left nothing for her to find. She must just be afraid that what happened to Jane and Edie will happen to me, like she was that first day they pulled Luce from the lake.

I lean back into her. Let her arms close around me. Everything is fine. "Thanks, Mom," I say. "I love you."

The church lot is so crowded that we have to park on the street. Everybody's here. Glen from the gas station, Dad's coworkers from the ranger station. Robbie, the bartender at Bullfrog's, wearing dark blue and checking his phone as he loiters in the shade. A carful of Bristow family friends is unloading by the walkway, Sheriff Marsden waiting to greet them. I pause for a moment to watch her shake hands and smile. Maybe she's just being polite, but I bet she's trying to get in good with the Salt Lake crowd, snag herself a spot on the fast track out of this county and onto something better.

Happy we could help.

"Wow," Dad says as we reach the church's front steps. "It's packed. Good thing you have an in with the hosts, huh?"

Mom elbows him in the ribs. "It's a funeral, Don."

"Not for another fifteen minutes or so." The smile he flashes me is conspiratorial, and usually I'd give him one back, but today that's more than I can manage.

"Come on," he says. "They set aside seats for us."

I wipe the sweat off my upper lip and follow him through the double doors, weaving between clusters of mourners as we pick a path down the aisle. White-painted walls, the pews scuffed and creaking. I don't see Luce anywhere yet. Hopefully she gets here soon so people can stare at her instead of me.

At last we reach the second row of pews, where a sheet of paper with our last name written on it is taped to the near end. Dad slides in. My chest goes tight as I sidestep after him, Mom so close behind me that I can feel her skirt brushing my leg.

I sit down, take a long, slow breath. The pew is cool against the backs of my thighs, and there's a small gust of air on my neck—Dad's already folded his program into a fan, Jane's distorted face smiling up at me as he waves it gently. I bet she'd love that.

The Bristows are set up on one side of the altar, speaking to an older couple who live farther down in the prefabs, while the Gales are across the aisle from them holding their own receiving line. The caskets must be in between, at the center of the altar, but it's almost impossible to see anything amidst all the flowers. Wreaths, bouquets, garlands draped over the podium, all in bright yellows and pinks. And set up on easels in front of the first row of pews, a portrait each for Jane and Edie.

The billboard. The T-shirts. The memorial wall in the lodge. I cannot fucking get away from them.

I lurch to my feet. This room is too small; everyone is too close. I hope this isn't what it feels like in those caskets. See, girls? You should've stayed where I put you. The canyon was a better resting place than this.

In an instant, Mom is standing, too, cradling my elbow. "Nan? What is it?"

The scent of a hundred lilies, dizzying, dull. Every eye in this church drawn to me, watching to see if I cry. All of it like pressure on a bruise, like a hand on my throat.

"Nothing. I'm fine." I disentangle myself from her. "I think I just need some air."

She tries to hide it, but I can see her grimace, and I know what she's thinking. Running out on the funeral only minutes after arriving, especially when nobody's seen much of me since the girls were found in the canyon—it wouldn't look good.

"How about we get in the receiving line?" she says. "There's a little more space to breathe there."

Reluctantly, I nod. I'm not exactly eager to get close to the caskets, or to face the girls' parents now that they know there's no hope, but it does look less crowded up by the front of the church. Besides, better to get it over with. It might make the ceremony easier.

I follow her out of the pew and up the aisle, aware of Dad's broad frame keeping close behind me. He went back to work so quickly after the girls were found, and I thought I didn't care, but having him here right now is more of a comfort to me than anything else.

The receiving line moves forward as we join it, bringing me nearer to the Bristows. "How does it work?" I ask my mom. "Do we just talk to them? Or is there something you're supposed to say?"

She kisses my forehead; I force myself to let her. "You can offer your condolences, if you want. But they'll just be glad to see you. You mean a lot to them."

Because I'm all that's left of their children. The people Edie and Jane would have grown up to be, the secrets they kept—everything lives in me now. And I've known that since the day I killed the girls, but it was easier to carry when I wasn't attending their funeral.

We step up another place, so I focus instead on the path the line is taking us down. It leads to the Bristows first before crossing to the Gales on the other side of the altar; I can't decide if that's better or worse than the alternative. Edie would like it, though. The finale, the last word. That was Edie all the way down, and I can see her, suddenly, like I've summoned her from the canyon deep. Called her up from the siphon, hauled her body home. Edie carved from salt, Edie with eyes rotted black and liquid. Edie who taught me to love her and want her and hated me for it in the end.

"Mom," I say under my breath. "Mom, I don't know if—"

It's too late. We're at the front of the line, and Mrs. Bristow is reaching for me, wrapping me up in a hug before my mother's even let me go.

"Oh, Nan," Mrs. Bristow says in my ear, "thank you so much for coming. I know Jane's happy you're here."

Her perfume is apple-green, so familiar that for a

moment I'm in the suite at the lodge again, squinting through the sun at the lake beyond the balcony. It's the scent Jane always wore. I'd know it anywhere.

"Thanks for having me," I say. It sounds ridiculous—this isn't a fucking party—so as she releases me, I add: "I'm so sorry. I really miss her."

Mrs. Bristow's chin crumples. She looks away, but not before I get a glimpse of fresh tears tracking down her cheeks. Mr. Bristow takes her hand.

"Listen," he starts, "I know it's not easy for any of us to talk about today. But we wanted to make sure we . . ." He trails off. The voices around us seem to go dull, to pound at my temples. "Thank you. Thank you very much for bringing the girls home."

A pop in my ears. Dead quiet, and then the roar of the waterfall in Devil's Eye. I can't find any words. They've all drowned alongside Edie and Jane, given in to the siphon's clutch.

"I'm sorry it ended up like this," Dad says. His palm comes to rest on my shoulder. "But it must be a relief to have some closure."

"A relief?" Mr. Bristow echoes, and I can see how poorly it's landed. I slip away from my parents, into the gap between the Bristows and the Gales. My mom can smooth that over on her own; this is hard enough for me already.

But my regret is immediate, because there they are: the caskets lined up like two twin beds. Jane on the left, Edie on the right, both all but hidden under blankets of flowers. As if the families are hoping that if you can't see the real shape of it, you won't ask what's inside.

I don't have to ask. I know. Empty space and as much of each girl's skeleton as they could string together, minus the samples they sent away for testing.

It's only bones, I tell myself. It's not really them. And still, I can't stop staring. Waiting for the caskets to creak open. For Edie and Jane to climb out, saying, What a good trick, Nan. You should've seen your face.

Easing closer, I reach for Edie's casket. I'm about to lay my hand flat against the lid—what if I can feel her heart beating? What if the canyon still wanted to give her back to me, like it did with Luce, and we just didn't give it enough time?—when I notice the table set up between Edie and Jane. White electric candles arranged in one corner, a basket in another, filled with cards and letters people have left in memory. The rest of the table is covered in little trinkets. Two coasters from Bullfrog's that Robbie must've brought. A pack of Edie's favorite gum and a ticket stub from last year's homecoming game at Jane's school.

And two pairs of earrings. Gold hoops, small and

delicate. Silver studs, a star and a moon. Jane's and Edie's from the day they died, stolen from the box under my bed and left here, on the altar, for everyone to see.

A cold wave breaks, pulls me under. Steals the breath from my lungs until it's not Edie's heart that I can feel but my own, thundering in my ears, the rhythm keeping time to a sweet little song: somebody knows, somebody knows, somebody knows what you did.

NOW

I cannot move. Can barely think through the haze of panic that's taken hold of me. Who knew I had those earrings? And not just that I had them, but where I kept them? Who would— Fuck, who is this, who is this, and what am I supposed to do now?

I close my eyes. Let it look like I'm mourning, catch my breath before I open them again. Whoever planted the earrings must be here at the funeral, which means they might be watching me. I can't give anything away. Not until I figure out what the hell is going on. Because yes, somebody knows. But that doesn't quite mean I've been caught.

To find the earrings and put them here, instead of taking them to the police—could it mean that whoever's behind this has as much to lose as I do? It would've been easy. The sheriff's right outside, holding court in the parking lot. One word, one hint, and I could be in the back of a cruiser with a pair of handcuffs cinched tight around my wrists.

But I'm not.

I look over my shoulder, at the sea of people in their funeral black. Which one of you am I meant to thank?

A stirring in the crowd interrupts me, back by the double doors where it's standing room only. Movement, a scuffle, and voices raised loud enough that even people in the first pew turn to see what's going on.

"Is everyone all right?" Mrs. Gale says.

I don't know, but whatever's happening, it's pulled focus and given me a chance. I palm the earrings. Slip them into my bag. If anybody noticed, I'll talk my way out of it.

Down by the double doors, the throng of people has thinned just enough that I can see the cause of all the commotion. Mr. Allard, in the middle of a heated conversation with one of the ushers. He must have just arrived; Luce probably came with him, but I don't see her anywhere.

". . . is here, so why shouldn't I get to come in?" Mr. Allard is asking. "Why shouldn't this be—"

"Sir, please," the usher says. "I really think we should go outside."

"What the hell for?"

The usher reaches out to steady him. "This is a hard time for everyone. The families would—"

"The families?" Mr. Allard bats the usher's hand away with a startling strength. "I deserve to be here as much as any of you. Get out of my way."

The usher must be another of the Bristow family friends, because anybody local would know a polite approach doesn't work with Luce's dad when he's like this. The bleariness in his eyes, the missed button on his shirt. The way his body sways even as he's standing still.

Someone should really go find Robbie, from Bullfrog's. He has plenty of practice handling Mr. Allard when he's had too much.

I step away from the caskets, eager to disappear into the cluster of my parents and the Bristows—the farther I can get from where I found the earrings, the better—but I've barely moved when my dad breaks from the group and starts toward Mr. Allard.

"Come on, Kent," he says, loud enough that the people crowding the aisle part to let him pass. "Are you serious? Today, of all days?"

Next to me, Mom shakes her head. Mutters, "Jesus Christ, Don," which makes Mrs. Bristow wince.

"This isn't your business," Mr. Allard says as my dad draws even with him, church pews hemming them in on either side. The two men are almost the same height, the same build. I remember sometimes when they were in uniform, leaving for work side by side, I couldn't tell them apart.

Now the difference is all too clear.

"You're making it my business, causing a scene like this," Dad says, disgusted. "Tell me you didn't drive here."

Mr. Allard's expression darkens. "I'm a grown fucking man. I don't need your—"

"Yeah, actually, you do if—"

"I drove." A voice from behind Mr. Allard. Calm, firm. I crane my neck to get a better look, and there she is. Luce, her arms crossed over her black dress as she eyes our fathers. "Can the two of you get a grip, please?"

I haven't seen her since the night Sheriff Marsden gave her the news about her mom. And I thought it would be there—grief stamped in circles under her eyes, pressing heavy on her shoulders, pouring from her mouth like smoke. But this Luce is no different from the girl I climbed the canyon with.

"I'm just trying to keep things under control," my dad tells her. "This is a funeral. People are here to mourn."

"Yeah, so am I," Mr. Allard growls. "They found my wife in that canyon, or did you forget?"

I can't explain it. Lilac rush, midnight at Devil's Eye.

One second I'm standing next to my mother, watching it all happen, and the next I'm on my back on the carpet, my head in Mom's lap as she bends over me.

"Nan? Can you hear me?"

I blink. Try to swallow but my mouth is too dry. "What happened?"

"Someone get her some water," a man says behind me. "And call the sheriff in here to make some room. It's too damn crowded."

"I think you fainted," Mom says. Her palm smoothing over my hair, her face pinched with worry. "How do you feel?"

Ignore the way my vision swims, blurs. Ignore the ache behind my eyes, because I had my bag a moment ago and now it's not in my hands. The earrings. The fucking earrings. If someone else found them—

"Mom, where's my bag?"

I try to sit up. She keeps me pinned with her hand on my shoulder. "It's right here, Nan. I've got it. Slow breaths now, honey. It's all gonna be okay."

"And Dad?"

"He's—" She breaks off, looking down the aisle to where I can hear Sheriff Marsden's voice, telling everyone to back up and make space.

"Mom?"

"He's fine. It's all fine."

Her smile is stunted, frail; I let it comfort me anyway, and shut my eyes.

Outside, my head resting on Mom's shoulder as we wait in a slice of shade for Marsden to finish scolding Dad. Muffled organ music is coming through the closed church doors; they're carrying on with the funeral inside. Making their speeches, singing their hymns. Pretending nothing happened even as they all pass gossip and rumors from pew to pew.

Fuck all of them. They didn't really know my girls. They have no idea who they're really mourning.

At least Dad's not the only one getting a talking-to. Mr. Allard is out here, too, accompanied by a few of Dad's ranger colleagues and some of the sheriff's officers. They're gathered by the far corner of the building, Mr. Allard braced against the wall while his onetime friends ask him what the hell he was thinking, coming here like this and making such a scene.

I slip the funeral program out of Mom's bag and fan myself with it. Sweat running behind my ear and down my neck, my black dress painfully hot to the touch. If I thought it was the heat that made me faint earlier, I don't anymore; it's far worse out here, but I feel steadier on my feet now that we're free of the crowd.

"Is Dad almost done?" I ask.

"They're still talking." Mom points toward the far end of the parking lot, where Marsden's cruiser is idling. Standing next to it are Dad and the sheriff, their bodies angled away from the church to keep the sun out of their eyes. "But yeah, almost, I think."

"And then we can leave?" I'm anxious to get home, to check my room and see if whoever stole the earrings from me left anything behind. Besides, as distracting as Mr. Allard was, someone could still notice I stole them back, and I'd rather not be here if that happens.

"I don't know," Mom says. A long, unsettled silence, her brow furrowed. Then: "Are you all right to wait here for a minute?"

"I'll be fine."

"I don't want to leave you alone if you—"

"Mom, I'm fine. I just got overwhelmed in there."

She sighs. Kisses the crown of my head. "Okay. I'll be right back."

She crosses the parking lot, making her way toward the cruiser. Sheriff Marsden looks up as Mom approaches. Shifts her stance, and for the first time today, I notice the gun hooked onto her uniform belt. She wasn't carrying one on our hike to the Eye, but she is now; she must know, just like I do, that there is so much more to be afraid of here than in the canyon.

I check over my shoulder. Mr. Allard and the rangers, surrounded by police. Nobody can hurt me. Except—where is Luce? I lost track of her after I fainted.

She must've gone inside to the funeral. I bet she'll do my reading. Take my place at the altar, paper over my love for the girls with her own.

When I face my parents again, they're already deep in a hushed, frantic argument, the sheriff a few paces away. If she's trying to eavesdrop, she doesn't need to. I could tell her exactly what Mom and Dad are fighting about without hearing a word of it. It's all right there in the open—in Mom's furtive look to make sure I haven't followed her, in Dad's gesture of surrender as he nods in my direction. It's what the fights are always about. Money and time and the way things should be, and underneath it all, my fault, my fault.

Mom must win, because it's Dad who finally breaks away. Storms off toward his truck, passing me without a word and leaving Mom to smooth things over with Sheriff Marsden. Their conversation is much shorter. Just a moment or two before Marsden smiles, her eyes finding mine.

"What do you say, Nan?" she calls across the lot. "You ready to get home?"

"I . . . yeah." Did Mom go over there to ask for permission to leave? Why would Dad be upset about that? "Mom?"

She waves me over. Strain showing in the lines around her mouth. I can feel it bearing down on me too.

"There you are," she says, even though I haven't gone anywhere. "You're gonna ride home with the sheriff."

My eyes dart back and forth between her and Marsden. "Excuse me?"

"I'll drive your father back to work."

Over an hour alone with the sheriff. Nowhere to hide, nobody to help me, the fucking earrings sitting in my bag just waiting to be discovered. I can't. Even if she doesn't ask a single question, I don't trust it won't all come spilling out of me anyway.

"But what about . . ." I flounder, searching for some excuse, something I can pretend to be afraid of, but as far as everyone knows, I'm safest with the sheriff. "Will I be home by myself?"

"Only for a minute," Mom says. "I'm just gonna drop him in Bryce. I won't be long."

"So then why can't I just go with you guys? I don't—"

"Nan, you're going with the sheriff. End of." She waits

for me to nod before letting herself soften. Leaning into me, almost a whisper: "I need a minute to talk to your dad alone. That's all. Okay? Sheriff Marsden will take good care of you, and I'll see you at home."

There is no chance to keep arguing. Her palm on my back, ushering me toward Marsden—her distracted goodbye as she goes off to join my dad.

"Well?" Sheriff Marsden asks. Golden badge, car keys in hand. "You ready?"

No.

"Do I get to ride shotgun?" I say. "Or do I have to sit in the back?"

"Technically, the back. And I'd have to cuff you." For a moment I can't tell if she's serious. Then the split and shine of her smile, all too wide, all too eager as she says, "But don't worry. I think this time we can make an exception."

I climb into the car, holding my bag so tightly that I can feel my pulse in my fingertips. Watch the church in the side mirror as Marsden starts the car, and for a moment I think I can see her—Luce wrapped in desert red, waving goodbye—but then we're pulling out of the parking lot, and it doesn't matter anymore.

THEN

A blue satin evening, all of Saltcedar gathered by the lake under strung-up lights for the lodge's annual end-of-summer party. All of Saltcedar except us—four girls at the top of the hill, Jane and Edie waiting while Luce fusses over my eyeliner.

"I told you I would do it for you," she says, using her thumbnail to scrape a stray black flake off my cheek. "Why didn't you wait?"

She's not actually asking, so I don't answer. Reach up to make sure my hair is still in place, the bun at the nape of my neck twisted tight. Then, reassured, shut my eyes and breathe deep to catch that familiar whiff of Jane's perfume.

It was like a picture when I saw them here. Standing

in the streetlight glow, their arms linked, legs long and tan. Jane in pink, Luce in green, and Edie in white. My girls waiting for me to join the line. To make us whole.

"Okay, you're done," Luce says. I open my eyes. "Just don't cry or you'll ruin it."

"I won't, I promise." Jane's the one who'll cry at anything, not me.

"Are we good to go or what?" Edie says. She's wandered a little farther down the street, the lakeshore glimmering at the foot of the hill. "We'll miss the fireworks."

"No, we won't," Jane says, laughing, as Luce steps back from me and tells Edie nicely to calm the fuck down.

"Okay, okay," I say. Love for them beating so loud in my chest that I swear the whole town can hear it. "Let's go before you all kill each other."

Down by the water, the air's sweet and heavy with citronella. The party ripples across the beach like an oil slick, one end marked by the dance floor and the DJ set up on the launch ramp, the other by the bar up on the deck at Bullfrog's. Between, people sit at plastic tables and watch the dancing. They wade into the shallows with their small children; they pile their paper plates high with free food from the buffet.

Most of our parents are out on the dance floor, losing

their shit to a song I don't recognize, so we've found a spot at the far end of the party, in the space under the overhang of the Bullfrog's deck. A group of other townie kids are gathered farther in, passing a bottle of stolen liquor between them. I've known most of them all my life, but sometimes I still forget their names.

"Okay, this is ridiculous," Edie says. She's sitting in the sand, her back against one of the deck joists. "She's been gone for ages."

"It's been five minutes," Jane says. "Ten, max."

As soon as we claimed our spot, Luce went off to get us some food. Edie offered to go with her, but she said she was fine on her own, so of course Edie's sulking about it.

"Fine," she says. "Ten minutes. It still doesn't take that long to go through a fucking buffet."

"I'm sure the line is just long," Jane says. The peacemaker, as always. This summer she's had to work twice as hard; I think these days Edie would set her own house on fire if it meant Luce would come to watch it burn.

If it were me Edie wanted, she wouldn't have to do any of that.

If it were me—

"How about I go look for her?" I say. "She could need help."

Jane raises her eyebrows. I know what she's thinking—Luce said she was fine, Luce never needs help, Luce will hate you for this—but Edie's nodding, and that's what counts.

"Yeah," she says, "go tell her to get her ass back here."

I get to my feet, stand stooped to keep from bumping my head on the deck above. "I mean, I don't think I'll tell her exactly that, but sure."

Except Luce is nowhere to be seen. She's not waiting in the buffet line. She's not caught in conversation with a fellow Conservancy volunteer, not laughing in the middle of the dance floor, and she's not down at the beach, helping a couple of tourists' toddlers build sandcastles.

I wander back along the party's edge, my confusion growing as I search for a glimpse of her red hair. It's not like she'll have found other people to hang out with; Luce is well-liked by kids in our year, even admired, but I don't think she's ever said more than two words to any of them.

Bullfrog's is ahead. I keep to the left, away from the water, from Edie and Jane. I can't go back with nothing.

This side of the restaurant is the main entrance, wooden steps leading from a trio of parking spaces up to the high porch. Usually it's busy, but today all the activity is on the deck, by the bar, leaving the porch free to be a staging ground. Cases of beer, loaned coolers overflowing with ice because the walk-in is full. Boxes of generic-brand snacks, of napkins and plastic cups. There'll be even more of it all in the Bullfrog's catering van, which someone's left parked with the back doors open.

A dish breaks somewhere inside the restaurant—staff busy running the bar, and a reminder that I'm somewhere I'm probably not supposed to be. I should go.

But before I can, I spot it through the van's front windows. That flash of red, like the first hint of sunset, darkened by the tinted glass. "Luce?" I call. "Is that you?"

For a moment, nothing, and then the swing of her green dress as she steps out from behind the van.

"Hi," she says cheerily. "Let me guess. Edie sent you to come find me."

I hesitate. There's something about her right now. An edge to her smile, the kind I recognize from watching her during math tests at school.

"Yeah," I say. "She wants to know what's taking so long. What are you doing back here?"

I'm expecting her to roll her eyes. Obviously I'm snagging us food without having to wait in line, she'll say. Then I'll help her open one of the snack boxes and we'll steal a few beers on our way out.

"Nothing," she says instead. Her smile widens, turns coy. "Let's go."

She crosses toward me, hooks her arm through mine and tugs me in tight so we're side by side. It's odd, for

Luce. More affection than I get from her most days, almost like she's trying to make someone jealous.

No, not almost. Exactly like that. I can't believe I didn't think of it sooner.

"Okay, who is it?" I ask her, voice kept low between us. "I won't tell anyone, I promise."

"I don't know what you're talking about."

She tries to guide me away, back to the party, but I stop short. My hand covering hers where it's closed around my wrist, our heads leaning in close.

"Oh, come on," I say, "you absolutely do. Is it someone from school?"

"Nan—"

"A tourist? Gross, Luce. Jane's the only hot one."

Anger in her eyes, striking on mine like flint to steel. Her grip on me tightens. "Can you drop it, please? You're being ridiculous."

"Wow," I tease, "whoever it is must be really embarrassing." I pull free of her, dodge her outstretched hand and backtrack toward the van, laughing. "Hello? You can come out now."

I can hear someone moving on the other side. Hurrying out of sight, around behind another parked car, but it's not quick enough. A sliver reflected in the side mirror—the back of a man's head, his light hair cut short, and the white point of his shirt's collar.

The figure ducks out of sight. Seconds that pass like centuries, and a bolt of bitter, lilac shock. By the time I think to call out, he's disappeared so completely that it's no use.

"Luce," I say, "who was that?" But she's already walking back toward the party. Red hair hanging long down her back, her body held tall and proud. "Hey, wait!"

Thankfully, she stops. Faces me as I hurry to catch up with her. "Yeah?"

"What's going on? Who was that guy?" And why did he look familiar? Tall, broad-shouldered, like someone our parents' age.

Luce's brow furrows. "What guy?"

"Behind the van. I saw him leaving."

She cranes her neck to peer past me. "You mean like one of the Bullfrog's staff?"

"No, not a— There was a guy back there with you, Luce. Come on. I know what I saw."

"Yeah," she says, clearly holding back laughter, "but you'd think I'd have noticed someone there with me, wouldn't you?"

"But—"

"Enough, Nan. Calm down." She puts her hand on my shoulder. Her laughter is gone; what's left behind is something carved from stone. "I have no fucking idea what you're talking about."

The lights from the party don't reach out here. The far end of the marina, where the lodge's houseboats are moored while they're not being rented. Stars caught in the still surface of the lake, the wooden dock rough beneath me as I sit on the edge, staring out at the canyon on the horizon.

I didn't follow Luce back to the party. Couldn't work up the nerve, the embarrassment too heavy. I wandered away from the crowd instead, going over and over what I saw. The man turning away, hurrying toward the far side of Bullfrog's. Maybe a hookup, maybe a friend, maybe whoever was texting her like—

I push the memory of yesterday down hard. Like nothing. Never mind. I don't know who it could've been. But I swear, someone was there with her.

Except Luce seemed just as sure when she denied it.

I could have it wrong. It was only a second's glimpse, and through glass, in a mirror at a terrible angle. It could've been a trick of the light. And why would Luce lie to me about something like this?

I sigh, drop my head into my hands. God, I can only imagine what she's telling Edie and Jane.

It was so weird, she'll say. Nan wouldn't let it go; she

freaked out. Why does it even matter to her anyway? It's really none of her business.

Well, at least out here alone I don't have to watch it happen. The end of everything, written across their faces, as they decide they're done with me.

"Hello?"

I push back a wave of fear at the sound of someone approaching. The whole reason I came down this way is I figured nobody else would. What now?

"Nan?"

I twist around, heart in my throat, to see a girl's silhouette poised at the other end of the dock. Face obscured in shadow, her dark hair painted floodlight white. She could be Edie at this distance, but I recognize that pink dress.

"Jane," I call back. "What are you doing out here?"

She starts down the dock toward me, slats creaking with every step. I bet Luce sent her to deliver the final blow—we don't want you anymore, Nan. We can't tolerate you another second.

But to my surprise, when she reaches the end of the dock, all she says is, "I wanted to check on you. Make sure you're okay."

"Really?"

She smiles and sits down next to me, feet dangling in

the water. "Yeah, really. Luce said your mom needed to talk to you?"

Is that how she explained my absence? Or is Jane just bullshitting to be nice? Either way, it's better than I expected, and I'm not about to argue.

"Yeah," I say. "Just some family stuff."

"I'm sorry. That can be tough."

We lapse into silence. Look out across the lake. In the distance I can see a light bobbing on the water. A houseboat moored near the center of the lake, people gathered on its rear deck. Later, when someone sets off fireworks from the beach, they'll have the perfect view. And in a week when summer's over, they'll get in their cars. Leave town and go home, and Jane will be one of them.

"Do you miss it here?" I ask her. "When you're in Salt Lake."

"Yeah," she says softly. "I really, really do."

I think of the other night, me and Edie watching the sky. Luce and Jane have plans, she said, and I'm sure that's true, but I think Jane would give them up if she had a choice.

"We miss you too," I tell her.

She straightens, eyes widening. "Right. That's actually part of why I came to find you. Luce has an idea. She wants to go to the canyon tonight."

Oh, thank God. My body goes light as air, veins rushing cold like the deep of the lake. I'm not surprised Luce didn't come invite me herself, but if it was her idea, that might mean I haven't ruined everything. Maybe I still have a chance.

"That sounds great," I say. "You and Edie can make it too?"

She nods. "It'll be fun. Midnight okay? We can meet back here, if you don't mind grabbing the skiff keys."

"Sure, I can do that."

"Cool." Jane gets to her feet, grins down at me. "I'll see you later, then."

I watch her go with a matching smile on my face. A trip into the canyon, climbing deep into Devil's Eye. All four of us on that little stone beach, staring up at the stars, breathing the orchid-sweet air.

I can't think of anything better.

NOW

The passenger seat in Marsden's cruiser is scorching. Black fabric soaking up the sunlight all afternoon, but I ignore the discomfort and settle in. The sooner I'm home, the better.

"Give it a second," Sheriff Marsden says from the driver's side as she cranks the AC as soon as the engine's rumbled to life. "We're lucky this one has a working system."

I told myself before I got in that I wouldn't say anything. The whole way home, not a word, because one person already knows what I did, and I'm not about to help make it two. But I can't help the line that slips out, straight from the script Luce would always use with anyone who did her a favor.

"You really didn't have to do this."

"Don't be silly. I'm here to help."

She actually sounds like she means it. Like she agreed to this to help me, and not just to get me alone. Bullshit. I know this game.

"Yeah," I say, "but you must have all kinds of important shit to do, and you're stuck giving me a ride instead. I appreciate it."

"You're very welcome," Marsden says. "But this kind of thing *is* important. I have to look after you girls the best I can. Our town's already lost enough."

Dust churning behind us, the horizon ahead. Our town, she said. At least twenty years between her and Saltcedar, but she still remembers the warren of tunnels under the canyon floor. She knows this place as well as I do.

So what does she make of it all, then? Of the bodies spat out the other end of the siphon, of Luce and her missing year? I've heard her ask questions, heard her deliver bad news like it's the morning paper, but I'm not sure I could tell you what she actually thinks about any of it.

"Do you believe her?" I ask. Too sudden, too loud.

Marsden doesn't seem startled, though. "Who, Luce?"

"Yeah. About her amnesia, or whatever."

"Well," the sheriff says slowly, "you've seen her X-rays.

That's a pretty big hit she took. You could lose a lot of function to something like that."

"That's not really an answer."

Marsden laughs. "No, it's not." Silence, just the rumble of the tires beneath us, until she clears her throat. "Here's how I think about it. If Luce really doesn't remember, okay. That's it, and we work from there." She reaches for the AC vents, aims them away from us to quiet them. "But if Luce *does* remember what happened to her, there's more to it, right? If I think she remembers, I have to ask myself why she'd lie to me about it."

I'm conscious, suddenly, of the sheriff watching me. Not directly—her eyes are still on the road—but whether I'm a reflection in her side mirror or a shape in her peripheral vision, Marsden is paying me almost all of her attention.

My scalp prickles with heat. I adjust my hold on my bag, check to make sure it's all the way shut, the earrings secure inside. "And? Why would she?"

"I think, for a lie like this, it would be about protecting someone she loves. A family member, or a friend."

A friend like me. What does it mean if that's the line Marsden is taking? What does she already know?

The earrings on the offering table, gleaming in the light of a dozen electric candles. Could she have put them there? Figured out what happened and realized there's nothing but Luce's word against mine? The two of them, deciding to smoke out a confession by any means necessary.

"I don't think Luce would lie," I say. Relax, Nan. Breathe in. If you believe it, Marsden will too. "I mean, once in eighth grade, Edie cheated off Luce in algebra and Luce is the one who told our teacher because she didn't want the curve ruined if—"

"You said something the other day."

I clamp my mouth shut. Realize too late I've been babbling.

"During our interview," Marsden continues. "In the staff room at the lodge."

When my dad was with me. But nobody's here now to stop this from going somewhere it shouldn't.

"Is this another interview?" I ask. "I'm not eighteen yet. You know that, right?"

"I know."

"So you really shouldn't be—"

"It's okay. You're not in trouble." I go still, relieved and surprised in equal measure. "And you don't have to tell me anything but I do have to ask you, Nan. Why did you mention Luce's dad?"

"What?"

"Mr. Allard. When I asked if there was anybody hanging around, anybody you didn't feel comfortable with, you mentioned Kent. Why did you do that?"

Because I needed a distraction. A lifeline. Because I knew it would make you look.

"I told you," I say. "He was . . . I don't know. They used to argue."

"About money? School?"

I shake my head. "Luce got straight As. There was nothing to argue about."

"Okay." Marsden shifts in her seat, seeming to weigh her words. "You told me that's what they fought about, though."

"No, I didn't."

"At the lodge, during our interview. Remember?"

Oh, shit. She's right; I did. It was bullshit, and I thought that meant it couldn't hurt me, meant I didn't have to be careful, but I should've paid more attention. I should've seen the trap I'd set for myself.

"It's okay," Marsden says gently. "Why did you mention her dad, Nan?"

"I don't know," I say. The road winking in and out, a black hole opening underneath me. Like an archway in the canyon wall, leading me down, down, down. "I'm sorry; I don't think I should . . . I don't know."

"How about this?" Marsden asks. "I'll tell you what I think the reason is. And then you can tell me if I'm right or not."

It's at least thirty miles to the lake still. Thirty more

miles in this car with the sheriff, all but alone on the road. As much as I don't want to, I should probably play along.

"Fine," I say. Stare out the window at the desert blurring past. "If you want."

I don't think she expected me to agree, because Marsden is quiet for a minute or two. I swear I feel the car slow down, like she's buying herself time. But then:

"You've lived across from the Allards your whole life. Your dad and Mr. Allard even worked together."

"So?"

"Well, they worked together until they didn't, right? Mr. Allard was fired. Did anyone ever tell you why?"

Not exactly, but I figured it out. It wasn't hard. "He was in bad shape after Mrs. Allard disappeared," I say. "The park didn't want him anymore."

"From what they told me, it was a little more than that," Marsden says. "There was a fight between your dad and Mr. Allard."

"You mean an argument?"

"I mean a fight, Nan. Mr. Allard got away with only a black eye, but the park infirmary said your dad might've fractured two of his ribs." She glances over at me, some shade of meaning in her eyes that I can't quite parse. "They're not sure. He refused to go to the hospital."

I don't remember ever seeing him in a state like that. But then, it would've been easy for him to hide it from me.

From Mom. Just stay at work until it's healed, and we'll never have to worry about him.

"Why do you think they would've fought like that?" Marsden says, filling the space I've left open. "A black eye, fractured ribs. They must have been pretty mad."

I press back into my seat. My thumbnail digging hard into the print on my little finger. Luce's habit, become mine. "I don't know."

"I was thinking about it. You all have been neighbors for a long time. If your mom and Mr. Allard got close—"

I nearly choke on my own breath. "Excuse me?"

"I could see your dad having a score to settle over that."

"My mom would never." Marsden has no idea what she's talking about. If she'd spent more than a minute with my mother, she would realize that.

"Maybe nothing happened, then. Maybe it just looked like something did."

How am I even supposed to respond to that? Imagining Mom with Mr. Allard seems fundamentally impossible. And harder still, somehow, if I try to understand how we got here from a question about Luce and her memory.

"Look," I say, "I really don't think that's what happened. But even if I decided to believe that it did, how would it have anything to do with Luce?"

Marsden's shoulder radio chirps; she dials the volume

down. She must think this is important, and meanwhile it's all I can do not to laugh, because as long as I'm not in the story she's telling, it can't ever be true.

"Go with me," she says. "Your mom and Mr. Allard got involved, but his wife found out. They argued, or she threatened to tell everyone. Something like that. So, he killed her, hid her body in the canyon."

I'm startled into silence. By her bluntness, yes, but by the word itself—*kill*. God, what a thing, to hear that word spoken aloud after I've spent a year holding it so close.

"After that," Marsden says, "your dad found out about the affair too." She holds up one hand, forestalling the complaint she thinks I'm about to make. "I know, I know, but I said go with me. He found out about the affair and they had their fight, but then it was over. Everything was settled and done. Until Luce got suspicious."

"Sure," I say indulgently. Marsden really thinks she's got it solved, doesn't she? "Then what?"

I can see how my tone hits her. The unease in her as she hesitates. Good. Why should I be the only one uncomfortable?

When Marsden continues, it's more slowly, her voice tempered. "If Luce thought she knew what happened to her mom, I think she would've confided in her friends. Edie and Jane. I think she would've told them everything, without realizing it was putting them in danger. And when her dad found out about it all, he had to kill those girls to keep his secrets from getting out."

"He didn't kill Luce, though."

"No. Not Luce."

I can see the sketch of her theory well enough to fill it in. "You think he held her somewhere all year instead of killing her? Because she's his daughter and he loves her?"

"I— Yeah, something like that." Marsden looks over at me. Sighs at whatever she reads on my face. "The man's whole family disappeared in the same year, Nan. And you're the one who brought him up in that interview. I think you did because you know what he's capable of."

Here it is. A way out. A place for all the blame. I want to tell Marsden she's got it exactly right. Tell her that's what happened; that's where Luce has been all this time, and she should turn the cruiser around so we can go back to the church and arrest Mr. Allard.

Even a day ago I might have done it. But today there are two pairs of earrings tucked in my bag. Somebody out there took them from under my bed. Somebody knows what happened—who I killed, maybe even where Luce has been—and they could call my bluff at any moment. Better not to tempt them.

"I don't know," I say. "I guess it's possible."

It's not enough for Marsden. "Come on, Nan," she

insists. "Don't you have anything to say? You're the one who really cared about those girls. You're the one who can stand up for them now."

Isn't that what I'm doing? Refusing to fold their story into Maggie Allard's, holding tight to my part in it all—it's the only way I have left to love them.

"Okay," I say. Whatever she needs to hear to leave me the hell alone and call this conversation closed. "I'll keep that in mind."

The prefabs are deserted when we roll through half an hour later. Driveways empty, houses dark. Most everybody is still at the funeral. I'll bet that afterward they head to Bullfrog's to swap stories. Or drive up to Bryce instead after leaving the church, make good use of the afternoon. A nice city dinner in their black Sunday best.

I wish some of them had skipped the whole thing. It's not that I'm frightened to be here alone, but—

I just wish. That's all.

"Want me to come in with you?" the sheriff says, like she can sense it. "Your parents shouldn't be far behind, but I can keep you company until they get here."

"I'm fine." Just a little longer. We're almost there. "You can let me out here, actually."

"Oh, it's no problem." I undo my seat belt anyway. A

dashboard light flicks on; Marsden raises her eyebrows. "You know we're still moving, right?"

Days ago I followed this same car down this same road, watched it pull into the Allards' driveway with bad news sitting shotgun. Today it's my own last name on the mailbox as Marsden throws the cruiser into park.

She leaves the engine running, though. Twists in her seat, leaning back against the driver's door. This is it, her last salvo. I don't have to sit here and let it hit me.

I grab my door handle, pull and throw my weight into it. It doesn't move. Locked. "Sheriff," I say as calmly as possible, "could you—"

"I understand the position you're in. Really. I'm not trying to make your life harder." She's using that voice all adults seem to have picked up somewhere, the one that's supposed to make me feel like she's finally leveling with me. She isn't; they never are. "So you don't have to tell me about Kent. I'll back off, if you can just answer one more question for me."

"I think the door's stuck."

"One more thing," she says, as if she hasn't heard me. "That's it."

"I should really get inside, actually." Quick, before the weight of the day becomes too much to carry. "Can you please unlock the door? It's kind of freaking me out being trapped."

Yes, I think, that's a threat. That's what I'll tell people if you don't let me out this very second. I'm just a child, alone and afraid, and Sheriff Marsden held me against my will.

A confused little smile tugs at Marsden's mouth. She reaches across me to the inside of my door. Presses the button to unlock it. Right there, exactly where it would be on any fucking car.

"Try now," she says.

My cheeks go hot. Embarrassment like a knife in my back as I fling the door open. "Thanks for the ride."

"No problem."

I get out of the car. Make sure I have my bag—please, let none of the earrings have fallen out—before slamming the door shut.

"Nan," the sheriff calls. I don't look. "Will you at least think about what I said?"

About all that bullshit?

"Sure," I lie, and head for the house.

NOW

Inside, the door locked behind me, my back pressed flat against it and my heart pounding. It's odd—I felt calm in Marsden's car, almost smug as I listened to her tell me her little story, but now that I'm alone again, all I can think about is how badly that could've gone.

It's all right, I tell myself. You got through it.

Yeah, I did, but there'll be worse to come if I'm not careful.

My bag vibrates against my hip; I jump. It's just my phone ringing, though, Mom's name on the screen. I take a deep breath before I answer.

"Yeah?"

"Hi, honey. Are you home yet?"

Her voice carries strangely. Crackling and filtered from

the speaker, but from the kitchen, too, as if she were here with me. I breathe deep, shut my eyes for a moment. It's only the heat getting to me. The stress, the exhaustion.

"I just got in," I say. "Are you on your way back?"

"I'm leaving Bryce now. Your father wanted me to tell you he's sorry he didn't say goodbye."

"That's okay."

"He's gonna try to switch his shifts tomorrow," Mom says. "I think it'll be good for us all to be home for a little longer. What do you think?"

I risk a look out the window. If Marsden is still parked in the driveway, I need Mom and Dad back here as fast as possible. But thankfully, her cruiser's gone. The street silent, the Allard house waiting on the other side.

Empty, and it will be for a while.

"Nan? Did you hear me?"

"Yeah," I say. "Fine. I have to go, Mom."

"Nan—"

"See you," I say, and hang up before she can argue.

That conversation with Marsden was a pile of bullshit, but it made one thing very clear to me—she has not given up. Which makes holding on to these earrings a liability. Anybody could have taken them from my room; anybody could know what they mean. So, if I'm smart, I'll get rid of them as soon as I can.

And I think I know the perfect place to do it.

Cross the street, track the long reach of my shadow. This way, it says, come this way, past the houses and into the desert. Out to the dust fields where Luce once broke a bird's neck. Where a girl like you could disappear.

I don't follow. Heat clinging to my skin, to the buttons on my pretty black dress. I lick sweat from my upper lip and continue up the Allards' driveway. Keep left, away from the door. Mulch cracks underfoot as I cut through the empty garden bed, the wood so dry I think it might catch fire in the sun. I round the corner and make for Luce's bedroom window. Jimmy it open like it's my own.

I hoist myself up on the sill. Swing my legs over, my skirt catching on a splinter in the casing, and slide down to the floor on the other side. After I've pulled the window shut behind me, I turn, survey the room. At first, it looks the same as it always did. Furniture in the same spots, desk stacked with books she snuck out of the school library. But nothing's quite right. Luce used to keep her things almost painfully neat. Now everything is in disarray. The dresser drawers half open, the bed unmade. Papers scattered across her desk, all covered in what looks like her handwriting.

A diary? Could she have written about her missing year? I pick up a sheet of paper eagerly. Find the first word

I can decipher and start reading, only to stop a moment later, my throat gone tight. It's a draft of a eulogy. For Edie or Jane—I'm not sure which.

"Sorry," I whisper, and put the paper back where I found it.

In fact, the longer I look, the more this mess seems like her grief come calling. On the dresser, Luce's hairbrush, strands caught in its teeth. On the floor, a magazine she must've taken from the Bristows' suite at the lodge, a photo of a Salt Lake mansion on the cover. In the creases of her bedsheets, the impression of her body left behind.

A whole life waiting for me with open arms. I have been tempted by it before, but this time I can think of something better to do than call it mine. Break it, burn it down, paint the ruins red. Plant the earrings here and let the blame for all of this crash down on her.

I'd have felt sorry for it last summer. But it's not my fault she couldn't fucking stay dead.

Luce has a little trinket dish on top of her dresser. I could hide the earrings there, nestle them in the coil of a necklace I've never seen her wear and hope it's too obvious for her to notice. But then, she could be the one who stole them from me, and if she is, she'll know too well what to look for.

Instead, I kneel at the edge of Luce's bed like I'm ready

to pray. If you stole them, Luce, then you remember what I did, and if you remember, you're a fool not to be more afraid of me.

Bend low, peer into the dark and run my hands along the underside of the bedframe searching for gaps. I can tuck the earrings in here somewhere; a police search would discover them, but Luce will never find them on her own. Besides, there's a sweet satisfaction in the symmetry of it. From under my bed to under hers. If I cannot keep them, this will have to do.

But there's a shape there, back by the wall. Something low, rectangular. Way too small to be for storage, and it's not like Luce is keeping a ton of other shit under here. So what's so special about this?

I reach for it. The carpet soft with dust, the bedframe sharp against my shoulder as my fingertips find the object's edge and pull it out.

Dread, sudden and staggering, leaving me cold. A little wooden box, turquoise set into the lid.

It's mine.

Count my breaths, keep them slow and steady as I sit back on my heels. Easy, Nan. The park must sell thousands of these every year. Luce could have bought her own. Except there's the ding on the corner from when I dropped it last year, and the chip in the fake turquoise that got the park cashier to lower the price by five bucks.

I can feel a hot flush of panic creeping down my neck, crawling under the edge of my shoulder blades and burrowing into the muscle beneath. The earrings in my bag—Edie's crescent moon hanging in the sky—my own face in the mirror as I try on Jane's gold hoops—

Luce stole the box. I can't imagine any other way it ends up here. She must have snuck into my bedroom just like I have hers, dug through everything I own until she found what I hold precious and secret and dear. And she would only have come looking if—

Fuck. She knows. Maybe her amnesia was a lie; maybe it started out real, only to fade the longer she spent at home again. Or the past could still be empty for her. If anybody could put this all together without their own memory to help, it would be Luce. Whatever the case, I think the girl I tried to kill knows what I did.

Is that what she's trying to tell me? First the earrings, now this? Did she hide the box under her bed, a mirror of where she found it, because she knew I'd come looking?

Reach for the box, dig my fingernails into the gap under the lid to pry it open. The lid pops. Inside, a pressed orchid, an enamel pin, and a phone.

I stare at it. The box is mine, yes, but that phone is Luce's from last summer. I recognize its lilac case. Remember returning it to her after she left it at work, remember searching her body for it after I hit her. It wasn't on her then, or back with the girls' things on the little stone beach. Later, when the police traced the girls' phones, Edie's and Jane's both disappeared into the canyon dead zone, but Luce's was at home, sitting on her nightstand like she'd never left.

So why did Luce put it here now?

My skin crawls, an itch burrowing deep. Pick it up, it tells me. Something's waiting for you.

I grab the phone, the plastic case cool against my palm. I'll try the code I know she was using last summer. If it doesn't unlock, then I move on.

But it does. The code reveals Luce's plain white screen and carefully organized icons. Like a half-waking dream, I watch over my own shoulder as I open her inbox. Messages from Edie and Jane right at the top, as if they sent them yesterday. And, bumped farther down, that unknown number.

It's not that I forgot about it—sitting on the edge of my bathtub, staring down at these same texts on this same phone. I just chose not to remember. Never mentioned the threats to the old sheriff or to Marsden. Never thought twice about cutting the dye out of my hair.

Well, I'll have to remember now. I think Luce is asking me to.

I tap through to the stranger's conversation. I didn't

recognize the number last year, and I still don't. But I'm braver now than I was. I have more of myself to lose.

I open the unknown number's contact, and I hit dial.

It rings for ages. On and on, so long and I think whoever was using the number last summer must have let go of it by now, until finally the line connects.

"Hello? Who is this?"

Like an uppercut splitting bone, like a light on in my front window. I know you, I think. I know my father's voice.

"Luce?" Dad says. "Either talk or hang the fuck up."

A buzzing in my ears, louder and louder. Yes, I know his voice, but I've never heard it like this before. I open my mouth, a hundred questions waiting to be asked—who are you, who are you, what's happening—but then a beep, and the call is over.

My hands go numb; the phone falls to the floor. That was him. I called Luce's stranger and Don Carver picked up. And if this number is his, then he sent those texts. He threatened Luce. He's the one—

This whole time—

A seam in the world splits open. Rushing through it, a voracious, endless fear. You don't know a thing, it tells me. You don't know what lives in your father's heart. You don't know what he might've passed down to yours.

But Luce does. She knows everything. She always has.

I pick the phone back up. Scroll through her contacts until I hit another local number, with the name listed as NC Call Me. NC. Nan Carver. First the earrings, then the wooden box, and now this, leading me to her.

I place the call, lift the speaker to my ear, and wait. This is probably a bad idea, but I am too far at sea; I will take anything, anything, that can help me find solid ground again.

After two rings, the line connects. "Nan," Luce says on the other end. "Took you long enough."

NOW

She tells me to meet her. I think I can guess where, but I still ask. Feel a shiver crawl down my spine as she says, "The Eye. For old times' sake."

Which old times are those? I used to know. I used to see it all, moments hung on the walls of some grand gallery. Now I stand in the road between our houses and can't remember which is which, Luce's amnesia become mine.

"All right," I tell her. Look down at my funeral black. There's a tear in the hem I must've got climbing into her bedroom. "I just have to change first."

"Don't." Her voice is startlingly urgent. "It'll make a prettier picture this way."

"What will?" I ask. But she's already hung up.

NOW

The lodge skiff is already anchored at the canyon arch when I arrive. Luce must've taken it here; I noticed it was missing from the marina, forcing me to take someone's two-seater rental. I promised, as I left, that I would bring it back. Now, as I tie my boat to the skiff and slip overboard, I'm not sure that's a promise I'll be able to keep. This Luce isn't a person I can predict. She's not the girl I knew.

But then, I've never known her at all, have I? Lies from last summer all coming undone. And even now I don't know where she's been for a year; I don't know if her amnesia was real, or, if it wasn't, why she didn't turn me over to the police the second she got back.

Maybe tonight she'll tell me. I start the climb to Devil's Eye. Wade through the dregs of the river until I've reached the flat of the path, where she's left behind footprints in the red mud. I follow them. Place my steps just as she placed hers, and let her lead me into the dark.

THEN

Waiting at the marina, the keys to the lodge's skiff in my pocket. It was so easy to swipe them from the front desk; I think the girls would've been proud if they'd seen it.

I was early getting here, so I didn't expect to find anyone waiting for me, but they must be on their way, right? I reach for my phone to check the time, only to remember I left it at home when I changed out of my dress after the party. Fantastic.

Finally, minutes later, three shapes come traipsing down the dock. Luce leading the way, Jane and Edie behind. If they were all walking down together, they could've picked me up on the way.

"Sorry we're late," Luce says as they approach. "Blame Edie."

It's a joke, obviously, but when I look at the girl in question, she's glowering—and not at Luce, but at me.

"I would never," I say. It doesn't seem to soothe her, so instead I hold up the keys. "Ready?"

Luce takes the keys as she brushes past me. "Yeah. Come on."

Forget about the tension at the party, I tell myself, and follow her to the boat. Forget about all of it. From here we're starting new.

NOW

The trail leads me deep into the cut. Up the same slot I climbed with Luce and Sheriff Marsden. Through the clearing we stopped in, and onward still, toward Devil's Eye. I haven't been this far north since last summer, and in the year since, the last section of trail has become overgrown, covered by tamarisk and cheatgrass. Here and there I can see places where Luce has left her mark—a crushed thistle or a broken branch. She can't be too far ahead of me.

At last, the path slinks down into a long, narrow gulley. Near the other end is the spot where Luce fell. Where I killed her, and where she did not die. I'm half expecting her to be waiting there, the canyon walls framing her just so. But I don't see her. And the entrance beckons, a natural breach in the rock that leads to the cavern beyond.

For a moment, I don't move. I could leave if I wanted to. Go back to the lake's edge and let this whole day disappear. I think I've done something like that before.

But if I don't face this, Luce will do it for me. I lay my hand against the rough stone. Shut my eyes and listen, as if for a heartbeat. Her voice calls to me instead. Last summer's ghost. A bad dream lullaby.

Come with us, she says. Come with us to Devil's Eye.

I duck through the entrance, holding my breath, and emerge into the cavern.

Dried out ferns tumble down from the ledges overhead. The walls, once plush with fresh moss and lichen, are left bare now, pale rock painted rose by the sunset that drifts through the split in the ceiling. Below me, the beach is wider than I remember it, new ground exposed by the shrunken swimming hole.

It is a shadow of itself. Dull, dead, except there's Luce, standing ankle-deep in the water, her eyes lit with a terrible, dagger-point joy and her smile sweet as a snakebite.

"Oh, good," she says as our eyes meet across the cavern. "You kept the dress on. I thought it would be nice if we matched."

Both of us in our funeral black. Desert dust streaked

down my skirt. A tear in hers near the hem, a fresh cut across her knee showing through.

"Well?" She waves me in. "Don't just stand there."

A familiar chime singing through me. Yes, I think, yes, I have done this before, and it draws me toward her, down the last of the trail onto the beach. The light off the water casts strange patterns across her cheek. Behind her, the sweep and curve of the cavern wall, a curtain hung for her stage.

I almost wish people were here watching. I could shut my eyes. Let the sound of their applause tell me what's real. But it's just her and me, and I've done my part. It's time for her to explain hers.

I follow the path down to the water. The stone beach shifts under my feet. Sunset scattershot across the surface of the Eye, obscuring the churn of the siphon down below as I wade into the shallows to where Luce is waiting.

"It's too bad it's not as nice as it was last summer," she says. She's only a few yards away from me, from the person she knows tried to kill her, but she doesn't seem afraid. She's busy frowning at the dried moss on the cavern wall. "Funny the difference a year makes, right?"

"Yeah. Sure." I'm too wrung out from this whole day to muster up any tact. "Luce, what the hell is going on?"

She lets out a bark of laughter. Reaches up to tighten her long, red ponytail as she says, "Going on with what?"

I hesitate. The earrings, the phone—earlier they seemed like a display, a message from Luce written in the sky, crowing, "I know more than you do." But seeing her face to face, I have to ask myself: What if those things are all she has? Just a collection in a wooden box, no story in her head to knit them together.

Go slow now, Nan. Just like with Marsden, and with the old sheriff. Nobody's caught you yet.

"With the funeral," I say. "Was it you who left the earrings?"

An endless, unbearable breath as she watches me with narrowed eyes. "Fine," she says at last. "We can start there."

Her voice is flat, plain. Almost bored, and it sends an itch skittering across my skin.

"Well?" I say. "Are you gonna answer me, or what?"

She raises her eyebrows. "You really need me to? Yes, Nan. That was me."

"How did you know—" Careful, careful. Don't give her anything for free. "Where did you find them?"

"We're doing it like this?" She sighs, restless, swinging her arms back and forth like she used to do before her races at swim meets. "Your room, a few days ago. You were watching the press conference by the lodge, so I went looking while you were out."

It catches me across the ribs. The sight of her that day,

astride her bike under the billboard. She'd already done it by then.

"It was my first real chance after the police sent me home," she continues. "I wasn't sure what I'd find, exactly, but I figured you'd have kept some sort of proof. You Carvers are the collecting kind."

You Carvers, like that should mean something to me—a flicker at the back of my mind, like it almost does—but louder and louder, brighter and brighter, that word. *Proof.* A siren blaring, a burst of fire against the black.

If that's what she was looking for, it must mean she knows—

"Proof of what?" I ask, because that's what's careful, that's what's wise, but Luce shakes her head, disappointed.

"Come on, Nan," she says. "I'm giving you a chance here. Own it. Take your spotlight."

I want to laugh. She's absurd, she's ridiculous, she's out of her mind, except I think she's right too. I did what I did. I do not regret it. And still I've had to spend a year burying the truth, biting my tongue. I sat at that vigil for the girls two weeks ago, watched my work fall apart without saying a damn thing.

Now here we are. Luce and me, and I might be fucked but I also might never be this free again.

"You remember," I say. "You remember what happened."

She smiles. Small and satisfied. "I never forgot."

Like a held breath let go, it sighs out of me. And for a moment I can see the shape of it all in the air between us. That night in the canyon and the year since. A scar, a dream, a weight we've carried together.

Where have you been all this time, Luce? Was it cold there in winter? Did you see my face in the dark?

"You killed them," she says. The moment breaks, all the ease dropping out of her. "You hit me. It hurt, Nan."

I stare at her, a little thrown. What does that have to do with anything? She was supposed to be dead and she isn't. Anything in between is meaningless. "I wasn't trying to hurt you."

Luce rolls her eyes. "No, just to kill me. That's much better."

Rage sparking across the surface of the Eye, the cavern walls crackling white. I don't understand her, joking about it like this. Or the earrings, the fucking tricks and puzzles like it's a game and not the most important thing I ever did.

"What are we doing here?" I ask. "What's this about for you?"

"What do you mean?" She blinks, a frown creasing her brow, her face the picture of confusion, but I don't buy it for a second.

"You knew I'd find the box under your bed, right? You left your phone so I'd see it, so I'd call you. You wanted me here and I'm here."

Sure enough, in an instant she's smiling again. "Yes, you are."

"What for, then?" I step toward her, the water lapping at my shins. "To talk in circles? To swap stories? It doesn't make sense. You're not—"

I break off. A familiar feeling rising, too big to be spoken, too sharp to be held. Everything I did, all that sacrifice, all that risk. If it hurt, Luce, if I hurt you, then why does it feel like it never touched you at all?

"I'm not what?" she prods.

"You're—"

"Not what?"

"You're not angry! Why aren't you angry at me?"

Quiet, only my own echo to be heard as Luce considers me. A twitch in her muscles like a rattlesnake's tail.

"I'm angry, Nan," she says. "Let me assure you. I am very fucking angry. Do you have any idea what it's been like to keep my mouth shut while you lie to everyone over and over again?"

Another flicker at the back of my mind, this one like the flit of a hummingbird, like the shine of a coin in a wishing fountain.

"About what happened?" I ask. "Can you really blame me for not confessing?"

"That's not what I mean," she says. Her anger is all too clear now; she's trembling with it, fists clenched. "About the girls, Nan. Your best friends, right? That's what you tell everyone. But it's bullshit."

I stare at her, more bewildered than upset. "No, it isn't."

"We invited you to hang out a few times one summer. That's not the same as being friends."

She's so insistent, so determined, but this isn't making sense. Maybe it's the wound I left on her head; maybe she's got everything mixed up.

"Look," I say as calmly as I can, "I know we all argued that night. Is that what you're thinking of? Because it doesn't mean our friendship was over."

Luce makes a noise I've never heard before. A swallowed scream, frustration ripped raw. "God, what is wrong with you? Is it just that you lied about us so often that you believe it now? Or do you really not understand?"

"Understand what? I live across the street from you, Luce. I've known you my whole life."

"And? What did we ever do together?"

She says it like she's caught me in a trap. I don't see how; there's plenty I remember, and I can show it all to her if that's what she needs.

"School," I say. "Hanging out in Jane's suite or in your room."

"What else? If we're best friends, what else?"

"The party at the end of summer." And there it is again, another flicker, another knock at a locked door just out of sight. A voice calling my name in the distance. I keep talking to drown it out. "Or when we'd meet on the lakeshore to walk home, or . . ."

That's it. Those are the only pieces I can find, now that I'm really, truly looking. A handful of stars in an otherwise empty sky.

That fight, our last night here. I've spent every day since furious with Edie for lying about me, for striking a match and setting a lifetime of friendship on fire.

But if this is all there ever was—

"No," I say, "no, hang on."

It's too late. I remember.

THEN

Devil's Eye is in bloom. Stone walls plush with fresh green moss, the air laced with the scent of the orchids that grow, translucent and stunted, along the waterfall's edge. I thought it would be drying out this close to the end of summer, but in fact it's more beautiful tonight than I ever imagined it could be.

A breeze flits down through the gap in the stone ceiling. Sends a ripple across the surface of the Eye, all the way to the shallows where I've waded in up to my knees. Edie and Jane went in right when we first got here, ducked under to wet their hair while Luce and I watched from the little stone beach. Now they're lying next to Luce, stretched out in their bikinis like there's sunlight to tan by. I've decided next time they go in, I'll go with them—the water's nice, and I'll try not to care if they tease me for wearing a one-piece.

"Nan," Edie says from behind me. "What are you doing?"

"What do you mean?"

"Aren't you gonna sit down?"

I swing one leg back and forth, watch the water eddy. "In a minute. It's nice like this."

"It's creepy, actually."

"Creepy?" I turn around. See that she's propped herself up on her elbows, her dark eyes intent on me.

"Yeah," she says. "Everybody else is relaxing and you're just—"

"Edie," Luce says, a clear warning, but Edie ignores it.

"You're just standing there," she continues. "Like you're . . . I don't know. Lurking."

I'm too stunned to have any real idea what to say. All I can manage is a sullen, "I'm not lurking."

"Well, it feels like it."

Jane reaches out, slaps Edie's hip lazily with the back of her hand. "Can you ease up, please? It's not a big deal."

"Yes, it is," Edie says. "This is one of our last nights of the summer. Why did we have to invite someone else?"

Someone else? Is that all I am? I bite back my response. She's only trying to start shit, her sad little crush on Luce burning a hole in her heart, and she knows I'm the easiest target.

"We invited Nan," Luce says quietly, "because we wanted to be nice. Are you being nice right now, Edie?"

A spasm of anger ripples through Edie's body. "By all means," she says, "keep talking to me like I'm five years old."

Luce sighs. "You're the one picking a fight, Edie."

"No, I'm not."

"You are."

"This isn't picking a fight!" Edie pushes herself up to sitting. "What, because I'm the only one willing to call this out, I get the fucking Luce Allard scolding?"

Jane peers up at me over her shoulder. My body is blocking most of her moonlight, but I think I see her wince, mouth an apology. I smile back. Probably better for both of us to stay quiet and let Luce handle Edie herself. She's what Edie's really pissed about, after all.

"I'm not scolding you," Luce says. "I'm just talking to you. That's it."

"Oh, come on. You're never just talking."

"Am I supposed to know what that means?"

"It means that whatever you say is what happens!" Edie's voice rings in the air like evensong. "You say how you feel and that's how we all feel. You say that we're bringing Nan and we bring Nan. It doesn't matter that nobody else wanted a fucking summer project. It—"

"Project?"

"She's full of shit," Luce tells me. "Ignore her."

But how can I? "What does that mean?"

"Nothing." Luce glares at Edie. "Stop it, okay?" Another warning, this one with a more dangerous edge. I wish Edie would listen. We're getting too close to somewhere we can't come back from. I can feel it in my body, in the air. The end of forever, coming in like a thunderstorm.

Edie doesn't even look embarrassed. She leans forward, wet hair sticking to her cheek. "She's a spare fucking part, Luce. She's obsessed with us."

For an instant the Eye turns to solid silver. The sky pours down through the split in the ceiling, a waterfall shot through with stars, as I watch Edie's face fracture like cracked glass.

"Don't call me that," I say. But she doesn't so much as look at me. Like I'm not even here, like I'm not even real.

"Wasn't the party enough?" she goes on. "You freaked him out. You got what you wanted. So why did we have to do this too?"

A riptide pulls me out from shore. It roars, it screams; it gathers and grows until I can feel it, a great black wave coming in. "I'm not obsessed."

Luce stands up, one hand out like she's keeping me at

bay. "Everybody calm down, okay? Edie, now is really not the time."

There's a weight to her words that I can't quite grasp. Edie, though—she sees it, she knows, and it makes her furious.

"Yes, it is," she insists, louder now, "because I know it's all part of your plan, or whatever, but I don't want to spend another second of my summer—"

"Edie—"

"Hanging out with some leech!"

It ricochets off the cavern walls, rattles my teeth. The black water rises behind me, taller still, every awful part of me pulled up from the depths.

"Take it back," I say. "Right now. Take it the fuck back."

Edie lifts her chin. At last, she looks at me. "Or what?"

I bite my lip so hard it bleeds. The wave is cresting, about to break. It will drown me if it does. It will end all of us.

What if I let it?

"Nan." A touch at my elbow. "Nan, hey."

I startle. Luce is here next to me, her fingertips uncomfortably cold against my skin. "Forget about her," she tells me. "She's just in a bad mood."

"But you heard what she said. Make her take it back. Make her apologize."

"It's not worth it, I promise." Luce nods to the opening

in the cavern wall, where the trail leads back out into the slot. "Come on, let's go outside for a minute."

Edie scoffs. Lies down again, shuts her eyes and breathes deep like she's trying to fall asleep. Next to her, Jane is silent, her cheeks flushed with embarrassment. No disagreement or apology to be heard from any of them.

You're all cowards, I think. You're cowards, and you've broken my fucking heart.

"Yeah, all right," I say. "I could use some fresh air."

The weight of the rock in my hand—the cut it leaves on my palm—the sound it makes when it hits the back of her skull.

You could've said sorry, I think as I watch Luce fall. Now you never will.

NOW

Water gone cold as midwinter, the air thick and sticking, like breathing fresh honey. The lie I told myself unravels, leaving room for the rest to come rushing in. Every forgotten awful word, every careless laugh, playing on a reel in my head.

"Right," Luce says. "So can we stop lying now? You weren't our friend. You were our fucking stalker."

It's odd. There's the strangest sound coming from behind my ribs. A mourning dove, I think, but louder, louder, and no—it's a human voice. My own voice, saying, You were never friends. Your dozen summers, your old stories. They never belonged to you.

"Last year," I manage to say. "You hung out with me. You invited me here. Why would you do that?"

"See, that's the problem," Luce says. "I keep thinking we're on the same page, and then you open your mouth and it's like, Oh, yeah. You have no clue what's going on."

"Don't I?" It's a bare nerve she's struck, something tender and wounded. The sting of it enough to wake me up, pull me in from where I've been set adrift. "I'm the reason we're here at all. I did this. I killed you."

"Well, you didn't," Luce says, "but okay."

Press the heels of my palms against my eyes, try to breathe into the black. Half my life just fell apart, only ruins left to make sense of, but I know I hit her. I know Edie and Jane are dead. So why isn't she?

I let my hands fall and blink as Devil's Eye fits back together, piece by piece. Luce's hair smeared like blood against the gathering dark.

I give up. I can't do this myself.

"We were here," I tell her. "You were dead when I left. And then you came back and you have messed everything up. Everything. So if I really have no clue, can't you fucking explain?"

"No, Nan, I can't. Make an effort. I'm not just gonna hand it to you."

Right. I should've expected that. She wouldn't even let Edie copy her homework when Edie missed school for her grandfather's funeral.

"I really don't know. I've tried to figure it out but I don't understand. I mean, you couldn't have been surviving out here in the canyon the whole time."

"True," she says, eyebrows raised. "So?"

She wants more from me. The only theory I can think of right now isn't mine, and is likely bullshit, but still, I have to try.

"The sheriff thinks you were with your dad," I say. I sound so exhausted that it almost makes me laugh. "She thinks you and the girls found out he killed your mom, so he killed the girls, spared you because you're his kid. Held you hostage or some shit instead."

"And then she thinks I escaped?"

"Probably." I shrug. It doesn't matter anyway, does it?

"Well," Luce says, "Marsden gets half credit. She's kind of got the right idea." Her smile broadens. School-picture-perfect. "But she's got the wrong guy."

THEN

They're waiting for me. That's all I can think, standing there over Luce, the rock I hit her with still clutched in my hand. Edie and Jane are waiting. I need to go back in. But there's blood on my shirt. Pooling around Luce's head, running down the canyon floor to reach my bare feet. I'll have to rinse it off so they don't see.

I drop the rock. Back away from Luce, each step turning her from the girl I knew to nothing but a body. To a problem to solve. If I let Edie and Jane come out here, if they see what I did, they will tell their parents. The police. Everyone.

The black wave crests high, blots out the moon. They'll die without seeing it again.

Back through the cavern entrance, hesitating in the

shadows that gather at the threshold before the trail slopes down to the water. Edie and Jane are on the beach where I left them, laid out side by side, but Jane must hear my footsteps, because she twists around. Waves and says, "Hey. You okay?"

I fold my hands over my stomach. I know the dark is hiding any proof of what I've done, but still.

"Yeah," I say. "Thanks."

"Where's Luce?"

Leech, when I only ever loved you. When I only ever cared.

It is so easy to lie.

"She said she'd be right back," I tell her. Slip my stained shirt off over my head, adjust the strap of my bathing suit. "I think I'm gonna get in again for a minute. Want to come?"

Edie ignores me, but Jane gets up. "Sure," she says, too enthusiastically. She must be feeling bad about earlier. "I will."

I leave my clothes by the entrance. Climb onto a small ledge over the Eye and peer down into the water. I think I can see the shape of the siphon—a hint of movement under the surface, on the far side of the pool by the cavern wall. Don't dive too deeply; that's what Luce said when we arrived here. The siphon is too strong. Its current will take hold of you if you get too close.

But Jane is not a Saltcedar girl. She doesn't know Devil's Eye like we do. I will lead her to the edge of a black hole and she'll step into it all by herself without a second thought. And when Edie goes to rescue her—Edie and her swim practices in the middle of winter, her damp hair freezing solid as she waits for the bus—she'll follow Jane deep enough that the siphon will take her too.

Three girls gone, and only me left to tell the story.

To tell the truth.

"I'll race you," I call to Jane. The Eye is waiting for us. I jump in.

NOW

I try to keep steady, to hold tough, but it's no use. "What do you mean, the wrong guy?"

Luce reaches toward me. For a moment I think she's going to touch my cheek, but instead she flicks something off the strap of my dress, into the water. A beetle, emerald green and writhing as it drowns.

"You found the box," she says. It takes me a second to understand, this afternoon seemingly centuries removed from the two of us right here, right now. "What else was in there?"

"The phone."

"Exactly. And what did you learn?"

The texts from a stranger. The number dialed, and my father on the other end of the line.

"You were talking to my dad," I say. Ignore the way it catches in my throat. "He was . . ."

"Threatening," Luce supplies. "That's the word you're looking for. He was threatening me."

I know that she's right. I read those messages myself, let the way they unsettled me lead me here to her. But I can't keep hold of it. He's my father. Lilac sweet and so well-loved.

"I don't understand why he'd do that," I say. "My dad's a good guy, okay?"

I'm expecting more of the same from Luce. Sharp sarcasm, laughter. Another wall I'll have to climb to get anywhere close to the truth. But her expression goes soft, her mouth slack with a genuine surprise.

"You still think so?" she asks.

Yes, yes, I do. I'm sure I do. Dad working weeks away from home to provide for his family. Dad sitting next to me across from Sheriff Marsden, protecting me from her probing questions. Dad at the funeral this afternoon, calming everybody down, handling Mr. Allard. The back of his head, the set of his shoulders as he walked. White shirt and light hair, like I've seen a hundred times before. Like I saw in the side mirror of a van outside Bullfrog's a summer ago.

I double over. Sick with dizziness, the water around me

heaving with a pulse of its own as I struggle to catch my breath. It was him. That was my dad last year at the party, talking to Luce away from everyone else, hiding from me when I drew near. And I could've recognized him. The pieces were all there; instead I chose to look away.

How could I have been so fucking oblivious?

Edie's voice in my head, half memory, half haunting: I really don't know, Nan. You tell me.

What else did I miss, then? Something between him and Luce, something he didn't want anyone to know about.

"Luce," I say, "was he . . . Were the two of you . . ."

I can't get the rest out. It's too awful, too frightening to say aloud. But I don't have to, thank God, because Luce is shaking her head, mouth twisted in distaste.

"Gross, Nan. No. It was him and my mom."

I stare at her. The world around me feels so fragile; anything beyond the smallest movement will make it shatter. "Your mom? Really?"

"It's called an affair," Luce says wryly. "People have them."

Yes, they do, but not my dad. He leaves and he comes home and they fight, my mother and my father, they argue late into the night, but it's not about their marriage. It's just money. Just life.

"I don't believe you," I say. "I mean, I think my mom would've found out by now. Or my dad would've told her, or . . . I don't know. Someone would've noticed, though."

"Someone did," she fires back. "Me."

The moment turns to stone. Cracks, crumbles, until I can see something glittering inside. I stay quiet.

"I only figured it out by accident," Luce says, more gently, "if that makes you feel any better. I was just looking for my mom. I wasn't trying to start anything. But she had another phone she was hiding, and there were all these messages with this random number."

"With my dad."

She nods. "It seemed like it'd been going on for years. On and off, that kind of thing. And I wanted to talk to her about it, you know? I had questions. I was fucking upset. But she was gone, and your dad wasn't. So I made do. It didn't go very well."

No, I'm sure it didn't. Luce searching for answers, pushing and pushing past what's wise, because there's nothing she can stand not knowing. Digging deep enough to earn those texts from my father in response.

You need to stay away, he said. I think he meant from me, to keep me from learning the truth. Would I have believed it if I had?

Probably not. I'm not even sure I do now.

"I still don't get it," I say. "What does this have to do with you and me? Or with where the hell you've been for a year?"

Luce steps closer, the Eye churning around her. "Everything," she says. "Nan, everything."

THEN

The canyon striped blue, moonlight pooling in the palm of my hand. My hair is still wet from the Eye, and it drips down my back. Soaks the bloodstains at the hem of my shirt, but it does not wash them out.

At last, footsteps in the distance. I've been waiting here so long, sitting on a low outcropping and counting the layers of stone in the canyon wall. Now I stand up. Dry my eyes, though I have not been crying, and wave to the shape emerging into the slot.

"Dad," I say. "Over here."

It was Edie's phone I used to call him. Took it from her clothes after she and Jane drowned. Carried it down to the arch where the lodge skiff is still moored, right where the dead zone in the canyon gives way. I need you, I said.

Devil's Eye. Please don't tell anyone. I hung up before he could say a word in return.

"Nan," he says, moving more quickly in my direction. "What the hell's going on?"

He's dressed oddly, a T-shirt and the button-up he wore to the party paired with sweatpants and hiking boots. Of course—he must've grabbed the first things he could find before rushing out here, all in a panic.

"I'm sorry," I say, and head toward him. The worst of it is farther up the slot behind me. I'm not ready for him to see that yet. "Did I wake Mom up too?"

"She's fine. She's asleep." Dad draws even with me. This close, I can see the ashen pallor of his skin, the worry creasing his brow. "You scared the shit out of me. Are you okay?"

"I'm okay."

"What are you doing all the way out here? By yourself? What— Oh my God." He grabs my shoulders, holds me still. He's noticed the stains on my shirt. "Is that blood? Are you hurt?"

I push his hands off me. If another person touches me tonight, I think I might scream. "I told you I'm okay."

"Then what's going on? On the phone you said—"

"Something happened," I tell him. "Something bad." That's it, Nan. See how it hits him, one piece at a time.

Dad swallows hard. "Bad how?"

"I think it'll be okay." Take a breath, wait for the racing of my pulse to call that a lie. It doesn't. "But I need your help."

"With what?" He looks around, eyes narrowed as he searches through the dark. Then, a strangled gasp. He's seen it. The body laid out behind me a few yards up the slot, face down in the dust. "Who is that?"

I don't answer. What would it sound like if I tried to say her name? Which voice is mine?

Dad pushes past me. Boots scraping against the stone as he hurries up the trail. "Hello?" I hear him call to the girl on the ground. "Can you hear me?"

This is it. This is when she dies. Not when I killed her an hour ago but now, when my father looks at her body and knows her name. If I wanted to, I could run from it. I could slip back into the Eye, and nothing would find me there. Not if I dove deep enough.

But what I want is something different. I turn and watch as my dad reaches Luce's side. He drops to his knees. "Oh, Nan," he says. "What did you do?"

NOW

"After you hit me," Luce says, "I don't know how long I was out. But when I woke up, you were gone. And your dad was there instead."

A swell of black behind my eyes, so strong my knees buckle. I can hear my heart beating. I can hear the canyon cracking open and the lake shrinking and the world ending, quietly, quietly.

I've gone over it so many times. Luce in the gulley, Edie and Jane in the Eye. Me in the boat waiting for sunrise—that's how it ended, only how did I get there? How did I move Luce's body all by myself and make her disappear?

I didn't.

"I thought he'd kill me, honestly," she says. "We'd been

going back and forth all summer. Things would've been easier for him with me out of the picture."

I stare at her, cling to the line of her as the cavern around me threatens to fade into nothing. Bile burbling in my throat, a memory coming with it. I will it back down, but it won't stop.

"I begged him," she continues, "and I talked about my mom, about how much she loved me. I promised I'd never say a word about what you did. I don't know what convinced him, exactly. But he let me live."

Yes, yes, he did. I grab on to it with both hands, hope pulling me upright. "He let you go?"

Luce's expression hardens. "No, Nan. That's not what I said." She is closer to me now. I can smell her shampoo. It's the same as it was that night. "You know the cabins in the national park? The ones by the visitors' center?"

Wooden walls, sloping green roofs, tucked amidst the trees. Ranger housing built a hundred years ago. Dad lives in one when he's on shift.

"Yeah," I say. "So?"

"There's a couple older cabins they don't use. They're not marked on the maps anymore. He kept me in one of those all year."

It's on the tip of my tongue—why should I believe you? All you've done since you came back is lie—but there are tears winding down her cheeks. Shining pink in the sunset as her body trembles. I have watched Luce all my life and I've never seen her like this.

"Kept you?" I say. "What does that mean?"

"It means captive. It means trapped."

"But he wouldn't do that."

"Wouldn't he?" Not anger in her eyes, but pity, the way you look at a dead deer on the side of the highway as you drive past. "Sometimes he forgot to bring me food."

"Stop."

"I'd get so hungry I could hardly see."

I can't take another second of this. "Stop it."

"There was no heating. I was practically hypothermic for a month."

"Luce, please—"

"Oh, sorry," she snaps. "Is it hard to hear? It wasn't very nice to live through either."

Gazes locked, the cavern frozen around us. Maybe this can be the end of it all. I'll never hear another word out of her mouth, and the truth can stay where it's been for a year—locked in a cabin, left for dead.

But I can't. The spell broken as I draw a long, shuddering breath. There are still things I need to know.

"How are you here, then?" Let her take it as a challenge. Prove it, Luce. Make me believe it, if you can.

She doesn't answer right away. A few wandering steps toward the beach, one hand twisting her ponytail into a knot before she lets it fall again. I circle away, deeper into the Eye, eager to put myself farther from the cavern entrance if it means I'm farther from her too.

"Your dad offered me a deal," she says at last. "If I stayed hidden for a while, and if I promised to keep everything a secret, he'd sneak me out of the country after it all blew over. Send me to Rome or Berlin or something."

Just like she always wanted. I guess it's a reasonable plan—nobody would've known her overseas, especially not if she laid low, dyed her hair and changed her name.

"That's a pretty good deal," I say. "You didn't take it?"

"I told him I did." She rolls her head to one side. Her neck cracks. "I was nice. I was patient. I waited for ages, until he trusted me. He even started leaving the cabin door unlocked. I mean, we were in the middle of the woods. I had nothing. Where was I gonna go, right?"

Wrong, I think, and I swear from her smile Luce is thinking the same thing.

"Then the morning of the vigil he came by. He told me what was happening later. It was freaking him out, and I could just tell, you know? I could feel it. He was changing his mind."

"About the deal?"

"About letting me live." I recoil, stricken, but Luce doesn't notice. Thumbnail pressed into the pad of her little finger, her eyes distant until they flash back to mine.

"So it had to be then. I hiked to the highway. It took me all fucking day but I made it. And then I caught the bus to Saltcedar."

"Nobody recognized you?"

"Hat and sunglasses. I stole them at the bus station." She grins. "Plus the bus driver was a thousand years old. I don't think he could see past the steering wheel. But I got off a stop early, just in case. Snuck into town the long way around so nobody would spot me until it was time."

Right. Time for the vigil, for her resurrection.

I tip my head back. Stare at the split in the cavern ceiling, the breadth of Luce's story washing over me. It is just what I'd expect of her, and at the same time, so beyond sense that I can't fit it all into my head.

Luce has always wanted out of Saltcedar more than anything. She'd have died for it; she almost did. And yes, I ruined all her grand future plans that night, but she still had a chance to leave behind the baggage, to get out free and clear. And last year's Luce would've taken it. What's done is done, she would've said. Take the prize no matter how.

"Something to say, Nan?" Luce asks from across the Eye. Singsong, mocking. "You're being awfully quiet."

"I just don't understand," I say. "Why would you come back like this? Why not take the deal, or even just go to the police the second you got free?"

"Right. The police, who practically consider your dad one of their own. I can take care of this myself, thanks."

Her smug little smile is enough to tip me over the edge. Past fear and past worry to my utter wit's end.

"Take care of what?" I snap. "All this bullshit because—what? My dad slept with your mom? You wanted him to send you to London instead of Rome? I mean, what is this, Luce, besides some big fucking spectacle?"

"A haunting." Quiet between us, sharp and whipcrack quick. "For you and Don Carver, so you never escape the people you killed."

THEN

"Listen to me," my father says. "Here is what has to happen now."

He's sat me down on a low ledge of stone. My bloodstained T-shirt balled up at his feet, his button-up wrapped around me.

"You need to be completely honest with me. I won't be angry. I just need to know everything. Do you understand?"

My hands are so cold. I can see them shaking but I cannot feel them. Were they always like that? I don't think they were.

"Nan? You with me? I know it's hard but you have to concentrate."

"I am," I say. "Sorry."

"It's okay." Dad clasps my hands. "Whose phone were you calling from? Luce's?"

"Edie's."

"Edie? Edie Gale?" A moment as he looks around, as if he's expecting her to step out of the shadows. "Where is it now?"

My mouth is dry. Cracked lips, bitter taste. "With her."

"Where's that? Nan? Where's that?"

"The siphon," I say. "In the Eye. Jane's there too."

"Jane Bristow?"

I nod.

"What were you doing out here with those girls?"

I do not answer, but Edie does. Obsessed, she says from the depths. You're a fucking leech, Nan. Isn't that right?

"Did Luce bring you here?" Dad squeezes my hands until they hurt. "Did . . . did she tell you something? About me?"

"Like what?"

"Never mind, sweetheart." He kisses my forehead. "It's all right."

I find his eyes in the dark. I know you. You are my father and you love me very much. "It is?"

"Yeah. If those girls went through the siphon, they're gone."

Unease stirs beneath my skin. "But what if—"

"Nobody's gonna find them. I promise."

"How do you know?"

"I just know."

"Dad—"

"Enough, Nan. I just do."

I want to let it go. Really. But I watch him kneel by Luce's body again, watch him turn it onto its back, and I can't.

"Dad," I say, "what could Luce have told me?"

He goes still. "What do you mean?"

"What you asked me before." I stand up, legs shaking, and he twists around to look at me. He's got her blood under his nails. "What were you talking about?"

"Nothing," he says. Silence, forever and forever. "Look, she just has some ideas, okay?"

"About what?"

"Me and . . ." I watch the anxious twitch of his fingers. "Me and her mom. But that's all they are. And I'm only telling you because you might hear some things after this, and I don't want you to get upset."

"Just ideas," I say slowly.

"Exactly, honey. They're not real." He smiles. "And we don't have to think about them anymore."

There is a shape hidden there. A picture, if I fit everything together. I think I recognize it; I think it looks like something dangerous.

I look at my dad instead. "Nobody will find the bodies?"

"Nobody. You have to trust me." He stands up, strokes my hair. His touch is too soft. "You trust me, don't you?"

There is only one answer. "Of course I do."

"Then I need you to focus on what I'm telling you. Right now Luce is our problem."

Yes. Luce.

"She's dead," I tell him. I have to make sure he understands.

He nods, and he says, "I know. It'll be okay, Nan. You did the right thing calling me." His silhouette against the sky, stars draped over his shoulders. "Don't worry. I'll take care of everything."

NOW

For me and Don Carver. Me and my dad, and the people we killed.

I remember everything. All of it, like floodwater filling the canyon. There he is, my father climbing up the trail. Kneeling over Luce, telling me not to worry. Telling me what's real.

I listened so well. Held on to only what I could bear and put everything else away in the quietest part of my mind. All my questions, all my doubt behind a seam sewn with fine white thread.

It's all undone now. Luce and I have picked out every stitch; we've torn it all open and I can see, now, what I worked hardest to forget. The kind of man my father is.

The lies he gave me to tell. The secrets he asked me to keep.

And I did it all willingly, because it meant I could go on loving him—believing in him—trusting him. Never mind the rock in my hand, Luce's blood on my shirt, and the girls drowning in the Eye. That was easy to carry, as long as I could leave behind the rest.

Yes, I did it all willingly. And he let me.

"He told me they'd never find any of you," I say in a voice that hardly sounds like mine. "He knew exactly what to do, because he'd done it before."

"To my mother." For a moment I'd swear it's Maggie Allard standing there, but in a blink Luce is herself again. "I don't think it was planned. She must've pissed him off. Maybe she tried to end it and he didn't want that. Or she could've threatened to tell everyone about the two of them. I don't know. But I saw their texts. They met up the night she disappeared. It was the last thing she ever did."

He would've carried her up here in spring. Runoff still fresh from the mountains, the water level higher without a summer of sun to dry it down. He wouldn't have left a trail.

I followed it anyway. I'm my father's daughter, after all.

"Do you see it now?" Luce says. "Do you understand?"

I find her eyes in the gathering dark. She is shining

with triumph, with a burnished rage. The best friend I never had. The girl I couldn't kill.

She smiles, eager. Hungry. Takes a step toward me, and suddenly, I'm aware of the strength in her body. Her tall frame, her muscles lean and alert.

I am not safe. I haven't been since the second I got here.

"That's why I came back this way," Luce says. "So you and your father see my face everywhere, for the rest of your lives." A tilt of her head, teeth bared. "However long they happen to be."

I shift toward the beach, slowly, so the ripples in the water don't give me away. I need to keep her talking until I can get a better line toward the exit. "What does that mean?"

Luce scoffs. "Take a guess."

I'm closer to the trail now. But at this angle she could still block my way out, even if I made a run for it. Think, Nan, think.

"It just seems like a waste," I say. "You go to all that trouble only to end up arrested? Didn't you think about how it would look, bringing me out here like this?"

"What are you talking about?" As I watch, her expression transforms, guileless and afraid. "I didn't bring you here. You brought me. Thank goodness I managed to call my dad before you took me. He probably went straight to the sheriff. I'll bet she's almost here."

Too late, I understand. It'll look to the police like I marched Luce out here. Like I threatened her, like I was ready to kill her to keep her from talking. All she has to do is claim self-defense, and anything she does to me now, she'll have grounds for.

I played right into her fucking hands.

"Wait," I say, but she's already coming toward me, the act dropped.

"This is the bottom line, Nan," she says. "You said earlier that when I came back, I messed everything up. Like all this was your story and I ruined the ending."

I retreat. Deeper into the Eye, until there's nowhere to go, until Luce is only a breath away.

"It's not your story, though. It's mine." She grabs a fistful of my hair. "And I'm fucking finishing it."

THEN

Until the sun is overhead. Until you have no shadow. That's how long you wait for them, my father told me. And I always do as he says.

I'm stretched out on the skiff's bench seat, staring up at the underside of the arch. Around me the canyon is silent. Still, too, as though it's holding its breath, waiting for morning. Strange. It seemed so loud up in the cut. I kept hearing the girls long after they died.

A gust of wind comes barreling down the canyon chute. Hits the water, stirring a small wave and stretching my mooring line taut. I'll cut it once the sun's up. Let it sink to the lakebed and tell anyone who asks we never had one to begin with. Someone had to stay behind to mind the boat, didn't they? And why shouldn't it be me? I'm the one who stole the keys from the lodge; I'm the one who'd take the fall if the boat got lost.

Careful, I remind myself. Dad said I shouldn't practice too much. He said it needs to sound fresh when I tell the police. And if I do it right, they'll believe me. He promises.

Just like he promised about the bodies, only I'm not supposed to think about that.

About what, Nan? a voice says from over the side of the boat.

I sit up. Crawl to the gunwale and peer into the water below. My own reflection looks up at me from the surface, her hair braided with watergrass, her smile minnow-quick.

Weren't you there for it? I ask her. Didn't you see?

No, my mirror-girl says. I do not go to Devil's Eye. Tell me what you remember—tell me what happened, and I will forget the rest. I will make it true for both of us.

I stare down at her face, at the emptiness of it. She has none of the questions I do. She did not hear the truth in Edie's voice; she did not wonder what her father might have done.

I would trade places with her if I could.

"They were my friends," I say into the quiet. "My best friends. And they loved me very much."

The sun is starting to rise. I finish the story. It's all over now.

NOW

Luce crashes into me. Pain rips down my scalp as she pulls my hair. Her forearm catching me across the throat, her knee cracking hard against my hip. I tumble backward into the Eye.

Water fills my mouth, my nose. Air bubbles rush past me. I can't see anything but the billow of my black dress. Move, Nan, move. You have to get away.

I push up to break the surface, knees ripping against the rocks. But I only manage one gasping breath. Then Luce is on me again, her arms hooked around my waist as the weight of her body knocks me sideways. I wrestle against her grip, elbow her in the gut. Bite down hard on the stretched tendons of her wrist until she cries out.

It's not enough. The water closes over my head.

We sink together, the current roiling in the depths, ready to keep and kill us. I stop fighting. Ignore the strain of my lungs and go limp in Luce's arms. We're close to the siphon now. When I die, it'll be like Edie and Jane. Does Luce know that? Is that why she's chosen this?

That's when she lets me go. Pushes away from me, her hair in a cloud around her. For a moment, the two of us hang suspended in the Eye. Luce's shape drifting above me.

Have we both died? Is it over? Did she follow me too far down?

But then: a strange glow on the surface, like a ray of sun. No—a flashlight. The muffled sound of voices. Silhouettes warped by the water, moving—

Diving—

Two figures cut cleanly through the Eye, strong strokes carrying them toward us. One swims for Luce, but the other knifes down to me. Sheriff Marsden, with her hand outstretched. I can hear her trying to yell my name.

If I reach for her, what am I choosing? Luce, laughing. My mother in tears, telling me she taught me better than this. My father in the news, my house empty and dark.

Below, the crush of the siphon. I could kick down, let it take me. Let it pull me through into the canyon heart, forget all the rest and spend my last ounce of breath calling for Edie and Jane. Praying they've waited for me, the way best friends should.

The siphon's mouth gapes wide. Summer in the canyon like heaven beyond, but Luce was right. That story is over now.

It's time, I think, and I reach up.

EPILOGUE

We'll invite her, to be nice, Luce tells Jane and Edie. A night near midsummer before any of it starts, the three of them in Jane's bedroom. We'll be good people; we'll be kind. I just think she could use a friend.

That isn't exactly true.

The aftermath is just what she hoped it would be. Luce does her interviews. She poses for cameras and she waves and she tears up so prettily at all the right moments. And when she gets back to the fancy new apartment she and her dad bought in Salt Lake, she stares at herself in the mirror and smiles. She won, after all. Nan and Don Carver are pending trial, stuck seeing her face wherever they go. The world is at her feet; this is how it was supposed to happen.

Still, there are things she never talks about. A night during her missing year, near Christmas, when Don brought her a hot meal and she hugged him and meant it. How it stung to open that wooden box under Nan's bed and see Edie's studs, Jane's hoops, and nothing of her own.

And the plan. The real plan for that last summer night, four girls together at Devil's Eye.

Don't tell Jane, she whispers to Edie over the phone the next morning. She won't like it. But it'll be so funny. We'll ditch Nan in the canyon. Just a little prank to freak her dad out. No, don't worry—she'll be totally fine.

That isn't exactly true either.

Luce can still see it. She can still hear the steps she used to recite like an evening prayer.

Become Nan's friend. Take her to Devil's Eye with Edie and Jane. Then, when it's been a little while, lead her somewhere private. Just the two of you. Look her in the eye and kill her with your bare hands.

This is how you hurt Don Carver, she would tell herself. He is too respected, too strong, too powerful to touch, but Nan? She is the part of him you can reach. Kill her and he will feel it; take from him just like he took from you.

It would have been perfect. It almost was, until Edie started talking and set Nan off. Luce hadn't expected that, but she thinks she made the best of it, all things considered.

Luce does her interviews. She wins her scholarships and she makes new plans for a new life and when she gets back to that fancy apartment, she smiles at her reflection. Oh well, she says. It would've been perfect, but you can't have everything.

Her reflection smiles back and says, Not yet.

ACKNOWLEDGMENTS

Writing *Kill Creatures* has been such a joy. Thank you to my agents, Daisy Parente, Jessica Mileo, and Kim Witherspoon, for your support in bringing this idea to fruition.

To my inimitable editor Krista Marino, as well as Lydia Gregovic and Emma Leynse—thank you so, so much for all your work on this book. Your feedback, patience, and encouragement are what allowed me to find the core of this story; I've been incredibly grateful to have your help.

To Ken Crossland for the interiors, Liz Dresner who designed the cover, and Kei-Ella Loewe who created the incredible art—thank you so much. I'm so in love with what you've created for this book.

Thank you, too, to Colleen Fellingham, Alison Kolani, Tamar Schwartz, Natalia Dextre, and the many others who so carefully shepherded this book through the production and publication process. To Joey Ho and Kathy Dunn in publicity, as well as to Kelly McGauley, Elizabeth Ward, Kristin Guy, and the larger RHCB marketing and publicity teams, thank you so much! You are beyond lovely and I count myself very lucky to get to work with you. Thank you as well to Joe English and the sales team; I am in constant awe of you all.

To the publishing team at Random House—Wendy Loggia, Gillian Levinson, Judith Haut, and Barbara Marcus—thank you for your guidance and support. To everyone at Lutyens & Rubinstein and Inkwell, and to Polly Lyall Grant and the whole team at Scholastic UK, thank you for helping this book find more readers around the world.

To my friends and family, who have been tirelessly supportive and unfailingly kind, I am so grateful to know you all. Thank you, Scallion the cat, for making me laugh. And thank you to the baristas at my local coffee shop, especially everyone who usually closes, for every medium iced oat caramel latte.

I have erred on the side of brevity here, but please know I appreciate you all more than I can say.

CONTENT WARNINGS FOR *KILL CREATURES*

Descriptions of physical violence and murder

Animal cruelty (animals involved are not pets, incidents are imagined or references rather than depictions)

Drowning

Gore, blood

References to alcohol and underage drinking, as well as implied alcoholism in a parent

References to prolonged captivity

Infidelity

Distortion and manipulation of memory/perception

This list is also available on the author's website, where it is kept updated to include any additional warnings suggested by readers.

ABOUT THE AUTHOR

Rory Power lives in Rhode Island and has an MA in prose fiction from the University of East Anglia. She is the *New York Times* bestselling author of *Wilder Girls*, *Burn Our Bodies Down*, and *Kill Creatures*, as well as *In a Garden Burning Gold* and its sequel, *In an Orchard Grown from Ash*, for adult readers.

itsrorypower.com